Ozma

Candace Robinson & Amber R. Duell

Edited by Tracy Auerbach
Cover Design by Covers by Juan

For SiriGuruDev

Chapter One

Ozma

Two Years Ago

Pumpkin innards slid through Tip's fingers as he swirled his palm around the carcass. He ripped the guts out, threw them in the grass at his feet, and pressed his digits back inside. The pungent odor wafted into his nostrils.

"I can think of a better use for your hands than that," a deep voice said from behind him.

Tip rolled his eyes and turned to face Jack with a grin. "The pumpkins are keeping them a bit pre-occupied at the moment." But they were itching to be somewhere else, *on* someone else.

Jack walked around Tip until he stood in front of him, his orange hair damp from his bath in the lake, his hazel irises greener than ever. Any lingering scent of Tip after they'd made love in Jack's hut had been washed away. Tip still needed to bathe himself, but why bother when he was required to gut pumpkins? Mombi had to make her pies for the market so there wasn't much time left.

They were well hidden on the side of Jack's hut, diagonally

across the field from the one Tip shared with Mombi. Both were the only homes within the witch's magic barrier, and Mombi's spells kept Tip and Jack from escaping. Tip had tried running away before, on numerous counts, and it was impossible.

Not taking his gaze from Jack's, Tip slowly pressed his hand inside the pumpkin. Jack swiped his tongue against his lower lip, took the fruit from Tip's hands, and set it to the side. Then Jack caged Tip against the hut and nudged Jack's nose gently with his own. Blood rushed straight to Tip's cock.

"Again?" Tip asked, inching closer to his lover.

"Again," Jack whispered, softly licking Tip's lips before pressing his mouth against his lover's in a starved kiss.

Greedily, Tip kissed Jack back and pulled him down to the ground. Bits of pumpkin smeared Jack's wet hair as he gripped it, making him dirty all over again.

Their mouths glided over one another, and Tip felt the firmness of Jack's back as he slid his hand up his tunic. A groan escaped Tip as Jack reached between his legs and stroked him over his pants. The rush, the feeling, he needed him.

"Turn over," Tip rasped, bringing them both forward.

"I like it when you're demanding." Jack grinned, kissing Tip right below the jaw.

Tip preferred when Jack mounted him, but there were moments, like these, where he *needed* to be inside Jack, desperately.

As Jack got onto his knees, he reached to unbuckle his pants and stilled, a glazed look appearing in his hazel eyes.

No. Not again. Tip sighed. He already knew there was nothing he could do to prevent Jack from leaving. Mombi enslaved his mind whenever she needed Jack to cross the barrier, and it terrified him and Tip.

"Jack, just be careful," Tip urged.

"I always am." Jack smiled, but it wasn't his real smile.

"I love you."

Jack didn't return the sentiment as he scowled at the patch, hurrying to gather some of the pumpkins they'd collected that morning. He then placed them into a crate, his body twitching with the need to perform Mombi's tasks.

"We'll get the fuck out of here one day," Jack finally said, peering over his shoulder. He released a heavy breath and headed off in the direction of the red-flowered trees, toward the barrier, to freedom for a little while. But Jack wasn't free, just as Tip wasn't. Jack had told him that he may be able to get out to run errands, but it didn't mean anything, because he was still a slave while doing it. As soon as he crossed the barrier, he was compelled to finish Mombi's tasks. He couldn't remember things clearly—it was as if his mind was in a fog.

Tip groaned as he sat up—his length had softened, but he still missed the feel of Jack's touch. He shoved his hand back into the pumpkin and finished cleaning it for Mombi. But his worry for Jack wouldn't relent, so he focused on the one memory, years ago, that had changed everything between them.

Tip picked a few small pumpkins from the patch and set them aside. A thrashing of footsteps caused him to glance up and catch a head full of bright orange hair. He stilled and watched as Jack entered the pumpkin patch, his lips red and swollen after running errands in town. Again. Tip wasn't as confident as Jack, always feeling like he didn't fit in his body, so how could he expect Jack to find him attractive when he didn't feel it himself? Blood coursed through Tip, and he felt it pumping at the vein on the side of his neck. He was angry. Hardly anything could make him truly angry. Not even Mombi. Not when she slapped him across his face, or when her nails bit into his flesh until he bled. Yet Jack's swollen lips once more had Tip's fists tightened and his jaw clenched.

Well, Tip was going to find a way out of his entrapment. And, when he did, Tip would be the only one making Jack's lips red.

"Here," Tip spat, picking up the shovel and throwing it into Jack's hands.

Jack didn't say anything, only narrowed his eyes at him. Tip had never let his emotions get to him this way, never been this harsh with Jack. But he didn't care.

Tip could feel Jack's eyes burning into his back as he headed out of the pumpkin patch and away from Mombi's hut. After a day of work, Tip always walked back to Mombi's. For sixteen years, he always had—he wasn't one to disobey. But now he would. He would break through her magic barrier somehow. That was a promise.

After he stepped over the last row of newly bloomed pumpkins—still not yet orange—Jack's hand clasped Tip's wrist and tugged him back to his chest. "Where are you going?"

"Out of this cage," Tip said sharply.

"Mombi's barrier won't allow it." The tone in Jack's voice was melancholic. Tip knew his entrapment bothered Jack because he had repeatedly said that Tip should be free to roam wherever he wished. Jack wasn't truly free either, though. Yet Tip was still envious that Jack could leave. Get touched, caressed.

Tip whirled around and pulled his arm out of Jack's grasp. "I'm going to go and get kissed."

Jack lifted a brow, a smirk slowly spreading into a smile. "I don't think so."

"And why not? You get kissed all the time when you run Mombi's errands." And who knows what else. He'd probably tumbled all of Loland judging by his rumpled state.

"Even if you could leave, you're too … innocent." Jack's smile still remained.

Tip narrowed his eyes, his fists shaking. "Not for much longer." He spun around and trudged toward the forest. "We can't all get pleasured on our way home."

A low growl came from behind him. Then Jack appeared in front of Tip, placing a hand at his chest to prevent him from walking away. "When I leave the barrier, Mombi's magic makes me forget—you know that. She can't have me telling anyone about you. All I know when I'm out there is that I need to deliver pumpkins or get her supplies and come back. I never choose *to go."*

"And yet you can stop to fondle someone?" Tip's voice came out high-pitched. "Every time?"

Jack smirked again, his freckles glinting under the afternoon light as he took a step back. "Oh, I see now."

"What do you see?"

"You're jealous."

"No, I'm not." Tip's cheeks heated. He'd overreacted and had given himself away. With each passing day, it had grown harder and harder to keep his feelings for Jack hidden.

Jack sighed and shifted closer, angling his face near Tip's. "When I'm out there, and my mind isn't clear, I search for dark hair and eyes as blue as the sky. No one's eyes are as bright as yours, Tip. No one's. I don't know why I'm looking for this fae, when I should only be running Mombi's errands." He paused, his hazel gaze latching on to Tip's. "All right, the first part was a lie, I know why. It's not them I kiss. It's you. It's always *you. But I'm not good enough for you."*

Jack turned away and started walking back toward his hut, leaving Tip with more questions than answers.

"You can't do that." He jogged up to Jack, grabbed his upper arm, and spun him around. Jack was at least a head taller than him as he peered up. Tip's chest heaved and his hands shakily clasped both Jack's cheeks, bringing him closer, their lips merely a hairsbreadth from touching one another's. It wasn't outspoken Jack who made the move first. It was Tip, innocent *and shy Tip.*

He pressed his lips to Jack's, more hard than gentle. Desperate. Hungry. Ravenous as his mouth moved over Jack's. Tip had known he loved Jack as soon as Mombi had first brought the orange-haired fae home when he and Jack were both younglings. There had never been anything brotherly in their relationship. Only a strong friendship, a bond, and whatever this was.

Together their lips caressed, together their tongues danced. When Tip pulled back, Jack's eyes were glazed and looked to be full of stars, just as his own had to be.

"All the times I've dreamt of that kiss, it was nothing like this," Jack rasped.

"Me either. This was much better."

Tip smiled at the memory and finished the second pumpkin. He took the fruit into his arms and walked them across the field to Mombi's hut.

As he entered her home, the scent of spices hit his nostrils, along with several rotten things. Possibly a dead faerie she'd let decay for days. Who knew what else she kept behind the protected barrier of her bedroom—no one could get through the door but her.

The strong smells signaled that it was another potion for the Wizard to pass off as his own creation. Mombi came scowling out of her room after Tip closed the door. Her gray hair was pulled into a bun, and deep lines were etched in her face, more so around her lips and eyes. The sort of magic she continued to use was draining her of life, arching her spine, hunching her shoulders. One day, Tip knew the dark magic would kill her. And he and Jack both eagerly awaited that day.

"It took you this long to clean two pumpkins?" Mombi ripped the fruit from his hands and smacked him hard across the cheek. His head swung to the side. The slap burned, but he was used to it.

The best thing to do was stay silent. He started to turn but Mombi grabbed his shoulder to halt him. "You didn't answer my question." Her dim blue eyes bored into him as she leaned closer and inhaled.

Tip held his breath, his heart beating wildly in his chest. His bath. He hadn't bathed before coming here. *Damn it.*

Mombi took a step back and slammed her hand against his cheek, harder than before, the sound reverberating through the entire hut. "You've been fucking the slave!" she shouted and moved back, swiping a clay jar off the table. It crashed to the floor and shattered.

Tip took a deep swallow and shook his head. "No, I haven't."

"You're lying. I *smell* him all over you."

"No." She would be able to hear his lie again, but he tried to keep his voice even. "I'm not lying."

Mombi stepped over the broken pieces of the jar and held

her arm out toward him. She tightened an invisible hand around his throat, her magic biting in, cutting off his air supply.

The magic continued to squeeze, and he clawed at the air, trying to get out of its wicked grasp. *Air.* He couldn't get any in, and he could feel his face turning red, his lips blue.

Tip was going to die. Mombi was going to kill him. He wouldn't be able to tell Jack goodbye. The last thing he'd told Jack was that he loved him. At least Jack knew Tip's feelings.

Something pulsed through Tip then. Love. More than love. A thrum of power he'd never felt. Tip's body shook, his skin glowing. *Glowing?* It was glittering with blue flecks, like stardust.

Mombi's eyes widened, her lips parting, and her grip on his throat dropped. She twirled her hand in the air, drawing up her magic, and shooting sparks of various colors at him. But none of it connected with his body.

An itch tore at his back, then built into something else, as though his skin were painlessly spreading. They broke from his flesh, ripping his tunic, freeing themselves. *Wings.* Bright blue, feathery wings. It didn't stop there. His body started *changing.* His black locks of hair grew long, to his waist, lightening to bright golden hues. Tip's body seemed to stretch, as if he were growing taller, the sleeves of his tunic and ends of his pants becoming shorter. At his chest, breasts formed beneath his shirt, and he gasped. His body shook and his eyes widened with fear, not understanding what in all of Oz was happening.

Mombi covered her mouth and hissed as she stared at him in horror. "Ozma," she growled. The horrified look on her face turned to rage and she jolted forward, knocking Tip to the floor.

Tip wrestled out from under her and stood back up. He'd lost hold of whatever power was there, his body weakening. A rush of magic came from Mombi as she rose, barreling straight for Tip's back, severing his wings. Pain rocketed through him and he let out a high-pitched cry.

That wasn't his voice at all, but a female's. Behind him hung a large oval mirror, and he took a glance at himself, while straining to breathe. Higher cheekbones, plumper lips. Nothing about himself looked like Tip at all, except the color of his irises. He was truly female.

Mombi hurled a ball of orange magic at the severed wings, burning them to ash. Tip didn't have time to mourn what had just happened, when the front door burst open. *Jack.* He was back. And he'd come to save him. But it wasn't his beloved. It was Oz. The only other individual who could cross Mombi's barrier.

"What have you done?" The Wizard seethed.

"What are you doing here?" Mombi snapped back.

"The slippers felt her curse break and whirled me here with their magic." He jabbed a finger in Tip's direction. "Now, explain!"

"You knew she couldn't be hidden forever," Mombi screeched. "With both Pastoria and Lurline dead, you should have killed her."

"You know I can't do that. Has her magic returned yet?" Oz moved toward them, his lips curled to show blackened teeth.

"Not all of it."

"Good." Oz shifted his cape to the side, revealing the silver slippers—flat and glistening—on his feet. "I suppose I should tell you that you're Ozma, born of Pastoria and Lurline. You're the true queen of Oz, but it will remain our little secret."

"Wh—what?" Tip croaked. Shock left him rooted in place. "I'm who?"

"No one … anymore," the Wizard answered.

With those words, Tip—Ozma—froze as a blast of coldness exploded around her. It was as if ice were slowly encasing her body. But it wasn't. Instead, she was falling through the floor of the hut. Falling and falling through wintry coldness, until she collapsed onto a hard surface. She was not in pain. The only thing that ached was her back, where her wings had lived for a few brief moments.

But that wasn't completely true. Because so did her heart.

That ached even worse.

Chapter Two

Jack

Two years later

The sun beat on Jack's bare back, sending rivulets of sweat down his spine. He did his best to ignore the heat as he cleared weeds from between pumpkins. His bucket was nearly full with invasive sprouts and he still had half a field to clear.

Jack leaned back on his heels, his knees digging into the soft dirt, and wiped his forehead with the back of his hand. This had been much faster when Tip was there to help. Or maybe it only seemed to be faster because of the company. The conversation. The stolen heated looks when Mombi was certain not to see. A promise of more when they were finished with their chores. His gaze traveled across the field to where a crystal-clear pond was hidden among the trees. Mombi had refused to let Tip into her hut until he washed the dirt off, which had given them both the perfect excuse for privacy every night.

Running a hand down his face, smearing dirt over his freckles, he choked back a wave of tears. It had been two years since Tip had died. No amount of crying would bring him back, but they *would* bring Mombi's wrath down on him. She could smell the grief on him, smell the salt of his sorrow, and he was supposed to have gotten over Tip. *Shit*—he was never supposed to have mourned in the first place.

If only it were that easy. If only he hadn't been about to ask Tip to marry him. If only he hadn't planned his entire future around the male he'd loved so much. Tip had been his first lover—the only true one of his life. But, when given the choice to leave, he'd run so recklessly that he was torn apart and eaten in the Shifting Sands. Jack rubbed at the ache in his chest. Why hadn't Tip said goodbye? *Why?* Tip could've at least given him *that…* He would've fought for him to stay, would've done anything. Or maybe he would've helped him figure out a way to get around the Sands because Tip deserved his freedom—even if it was without Jack. His goodbye wouldn't have made a difference in the long run either way, but at least he could've asked Tip why he didn't love him anymore.

Jack stood slowly and carried the bucket toward the magical barrier. When he was close enough, he chucked the contents to the other side and swiveled toward his small hut instead of going straight back to work. He couldn't drown his heartache with tears, so he would drown it with something else.

Jars of pumpkin ale lined more shelves in his pitifully small pantry than food did. There was a wedge of cheese from his last trip to the market and half a loaf of bread, along with a couple glass jars filled with vegetables. Meat was a rare pleasure and he'd eaten so much pumpkin that the thought of eating more made him want to vomit—though he had to force it down to survive. *Tip would want me to live*, he thought. Even if he chose not to live alongside him. Besides, the ale distracted him from his hunger most of the time.

The lump in his throat worked furiously as he gulped down an entire jar. Jack's blood instantly warmed. The ale tasted like shit as it slid over his tongue, but it was oh-so wonderful. It made him forget there was a Tip-sized hole in his heart.

Almost.

With a low, pained scream, he hurled the clay jar across the hut. It hit the wall over his bed, *cracked*, and shattered. Shards scattered over the thin woven blanket on his bed. The bed he and Tip would fuck in when Mombi went to town alone, or when she was holed up in her hut working on potions.

"Why?" he mumbled to himself as he slid down the wall. "Why did you have to die? Why did you leave me here all alone?"

Why did you make me love you?

Jack didn't voice the last question because it was unfair. Tip hadn't *made* him fall in love—he'd simply been himself. Kind and funny and generous. If Tip lived in town, everyone would've loved him. Jack felt beyond lucky to have had Tip love him back, even if it was only for a little while. But *damn*. It hurt. It hurt so much he thought he would die too. Day after day after fucking day. For two years. He thought the pain would lessen over time, but it hadn't.

So why did you leave *me?*

Maybe Jack was the problem. His parents had left him too, after all. They'd placed him beneath a tree on the side of the road and told him to wait there. Three days later, Mombi had found him. Stolen him away to be her *thing*. The only affection he'd ever received was from Tip, but they were the same in that way. Mombi loathed them both. If he and Jack hadn't loved each other, no one would have. Perhaps that was why Tip left. To find someone to love for more than convenience. Could Jack blame him for that?

No.

Yes.

It was easier to drown out the question with his ale than decide which answer was true. Ale and fae. Whores, mostly. Whoever he could find with dark hair and blue eyes when he finished with Mombi's errands. Males or females, tall or short, horned or covered in scales. It didn't matter. None of it mattered as long as they resembled Tip. But none of them were *him*. They were each simply a way to forget for a moment—now that Mombi no longer made Jack forget his life on the farm when he left, compelled. There was no reason to keep Tip a secret now that he was dead—not that he understood the reasoning when his lover was alive.

Fucking heartless bitch.

"Jack!" Mombi screeched outside, pulling him from his thoughts. "I see your bucket—I know you're in there."

He sighed and rested his head against the wall behind him. There was no point hiding from the witch. The barrier trapped him on the farm unless Mombi sent him out to do her bidding—selling pumpkin pies and cakes and soups. Buying bread and seeds and eggs. Acquiring herbs for potions and bottles to put them in. But without her intentionally letting Jack out, there was nowhere for him to go.

"Get out here!"

I'll come out there and bash you over the head with a pumpkin, you evil bitch.

Jack shoved himself off the ground and stumbled. Perhaps drinking the entire jar in one go was a bad idea … but today was a bad day. Not that any of them were *good* anymore. Sometimes he just woke up feeling worse than others. Perhaps it had something to do with the dreams he had—if they included Tip or not.

"What?" he snapped, pushing through his door.

Mombi leaned on her cane at the edge of the pumpkin patch. Her hair had turned from gray to white over the last two years and thinned considerably. The wrinkles deepened around her mouth, and her back had become so hunched that she appeared nearly bent in half. If only her magic had withered as much as her body had, then maybe Jack could've escaped her barrier. There was no reason to stay—nothing keeping him there except for Mombi's barrier. By the looks of her, she wouldn't live much longer if she continued dabbling in dark spells.

Old hag.

Sharp pain lanced across Jack's chest and he yelped. A red welt swelled from his right shoulder down to his left hip where her magic struck.

"Watch your tone," Mombi warned. "Go finish those weeds, slave, or I'll slice off a patch of skin."

Ooh, more threats. What the hell else is new?

But even the alcohol couldn't bring Jack to say that aloud. The punishment would be far too severe. So, he bit his tongue and stumbled over to pick up his bucket.

"You're good for nothing," she mumbled. "Tip never gave me these problems."

Jack blanched at the mention of Tip's name. Mombi brought it up just to be a bitch and it never failed to give her the reaction she wanted. Tip had always been one to follow the rules… To keep him in line. It felt nearly impossible to do on his own. Everything did. He sighed silently and turned away from her.

"When you're finished, come to my hut," Mombi said to his back.

Jack's shoulders stiffened. That was never good. "Why?"

The wooden cane cracked against his lower leg and he winced at the pain.

"Don't question me."

If Mombi didn't want to tell him her reasoning, he wasn't going to change her mind. "All right," he said and returned to the same chores he'd done a million times. Over and over. Day after day.

Hours later, with the field clear of any unwanted growth, Jack tossed the empty bucket in the work shed. It landed with a loud clatter and knocked over a rake, which sent pouches of pumpkin seeds tumbling from a shelf. He dug his fists into his aching lower back and the thought of leaning over to collect them filled him with dread. It would be a miracle if he was able to stand again after an entire day on his knees. Besides, he was expected at Mombi's hut. *Damn witch.*

"Tomorrow," he said to no one. The seeds were sealed and it wasn't like they would go anywhere.

He shut and locked the shed, pocketing the keys. Mombi would demand that he give them back now that his work was done. Likely so Jack wouldn't get any ideas about murdering her with a trowel in the middle of the night. Not that he hadn't imagined it before. A trowel, a spade, a cultivator… If they had it, he'd dreamt of killing the witch with it. The only thing holding him back was the barrier and what would happen to it—to him and, once, Tip—if she died. Would they be trapped inside forever? Her spells weren't made using normal fae magic.

Jack sighed again and turned toward the hut on the other side of the field. *Might as well get it over with.*

Trudging toward Mombi's, he kicked at the pumpkin leaves that crept over onto the grass. Maybe he should've stopped for another jar of alcohol first. His mind was too clear now, his tongue feeling too sharp. Deep down, he knew he was about to get himself in trouble. Trouble that Tip would've been able to talk him out of creating. But Tip was dead. Jack knocked loudly on Mombi's door and it instantly swung open. The witch poked him hard in the chest with the end of her cane.

Poke me again and you'll find that cane shoved so far up your—

"Get the wagon," she snapped.

Jack ground his teeth together. He'd *just* been at the shed beside the maroon and blue wagon, the bed of it covered in curving wood, forming an arc, but he returned for it without a word. Mombi usually moved it with her magic until she located the stag she'd enchanted. How the hell was he supposed to push it on his own? Even if she'd had the damn thing when Tip was alive, the two of them wouldn't have been able to move it together.

Jack went behind the wagon and pushed with his shoulder. *Yeah-fucking-right.* Then he tried pulling from the front, digging his heels into the dirt, but it didn't budge. Finally, heaving from exertion, he stomped back to Mombi. "Look," he said more harshly than was smart. "That's not moving unless I get some help."

"You're pathetic. Always have been." Mombi tossed a fabric bag at his face.

He caught it with an *oomph.* "Pathetic or not, your wagon's not going anywhere unless you do it yourself."

The witch grumbled under her breath and shot a streak of yellow magic across the field. It hit the wagon with a small *crack.* Mombi circled her hand in the air, reeling the wagon up to the hut in less time than it had taken Jack to attempt the same thing.

"Load my belongings," she barked when it creaked to a stop in front of the hut. "Quickly now."

Jack opened the back of the wagon and set the bag inside. "Are we going somewhere?" he asked, his brow furrowing.

"I'm leaving." She disappeared into the hut and glass clinked together. "Dorothy has returned to Oz and I have to help the Wizard prepare."

Dorothy? Who the fuck was that and what did she have to do with Oz?

"What are you waiting for?" she snapped.

Jack hurried to grab a large trunk and heaved it out to the wagon. Mombi was leaving? For how long? Did that mean he was free? His mind spun and spun with possibilities. Even if she was only leaving for a short time, he would be alone. He would be *free of her.* For more than a handful of hours.

"When will you be back?" Jack asked hesitantly. His palms sweated with anticipation—if she was gone long enough, he could *really* examine the barrier for a weakness. Maybe he could escape too.

"When that little bitch is dead."

That didn't explain a damn thing about how long it would take. "What should I do?"

"What you always do!" she cried so loudly that her voice

cracked. "Do I have to tell you how to breathe? How to shit? Oz have mercy, you're not a youngling anymore. Even then, you were always *pitiful.*" Mombi hobbled out of the hut and slammed the door behind her. She set a crate full of jingling glass containers on top of her trunk and used her magic to push the wagon toward the barrier. "Where is that damn stag? I'm not pulling this wagon the whole journey myself!"

Probably looking for a hunter's trap so it doesn't have to drag your ass across Loland.

"I haven't seen him," Jack said. He'd only seen the stag a handful of times, and never on the farm. Mombi always released him outside the barrier, enchanted him to return when she needed him, then hauled the wagon home with her magic.

Mombi grumbled to herself and sent out a small burst of power. To call the stag, Jack assumed, but he didn't question it. His mind was too busy racing over the possibilities before him. Of what it could mean. Unless she never returned and he couldn't find a way to escape… He swallowed nervously.

Pulse racing, Jack watched her walk through the barrier. As much as he hated her, he didn't want to die on this farm. Alone. Trapped. The further Mombi got, the faster his heart thumped. *Fuck! I do* not *want to become pumpkin fertilizer.* Perhaps it wasn't too late to call out and offer his services. She could enchant him to help with this Dorothy and then he would be outside the barrier. The chances for escape would be greater… But then he would be stuck at Mombi's side for who knows how long.

Before he could make a decision, a shimmer of magic rippled over the pumpkin patch, disintegrating the spell that held him captive. The invisible cage was gone. His jaw dropped in disbelief. "What the fuck just happened?"

Chapter Three

Ozma

Present Day

Free. Ozma was free. She'd never known what that meant. All her life she'd belonged to Mombi, or had been a prisoner in the dark place with Reva—the Good Witch of the West who had been forced into becoming the Wicked Witch for a time. Trapped within Mombi's magical barrier around a small pumpkin farm in Loland, Ozma had never been able to venture out into the rest of Oz. There was a possibility that she could get stuck inside the barrier of the patch again, but she would try to get Jack's attention from outside it.

Loland was on the outskirts of the Shifting Sands, across from the Eastern Land of Oz. The Wizard had used the silver slippers to send her to the dark place, but Ozma was unsure how and when she'd been changed into Tip. But it had to have been sometime as a baby, because Reva had never known King Pastoria and Queen Lurline to have had a child. Her guess was that Mombi or Oz had stolen her, but then what? Why hadn't her parents gone searching for her or spread word that she'd gone missing before they'd died? She'd learned from Reva that Langwidere had taken Lurline's head and Oz had murdered Pastoria. That made Ozma the rightful ruler of Oz, and she had never known, not until she'd been angry enough to somehow break the curse that Mombi placed on her.

Ozma was going to kill them both, retrieve her slippers, and then her kingdom.

Seeing the world as it truly was, not from Jack's maps or Reva's stories, was no comparison. And it was nothing like the dark place—that nightmare world where only a mad dash and a climb to the tops of the tallest trees brought a moment's relief from the threatening creatures. The South had been deserted but it was still beautiful, and she'd come across live Wheelers! Killed one. Felt that rush of doing something good. She'd been inside a brothel with Reva, seen fae pleasuring one another out in the open. It had given her a shock, but also made her want to know more, understand how she might bring pleasure to Jack in this female body. She'd never even explored it much herself because of the constant danger in the dark place, and the endless running. Jack had always been attracted to males and females, while she had only ever been attracted to Jack. Though, she supposed, he was the only fae she had ever been around.

Since parting ways with Reva at the brothel, and waiting around to make sure Crow—Reva's husband—could catch up with her friend, Ozma had only stopped to rest in the branches of trees for the night. But she hadn't slept much. She wanted to stay awake not only to be prepared to run if need be, but to see the Land of Oz in the moonlight.

Ozma adjusted the blue dress she'd gotten from an abandoned shop with Reva before they'd left the South. She hopped over a rotting log, then another, the map of the vast land pulsing through her veins. Though Ozma didn't have her magic, something was there, guiding her in the right direction. The moment when Thelia's power had brought Ozma and Reva back from the dark place, she'd felt every inch of Oz within her.

Perhaps this was a bit of magic. She wanted to explore everything, but not yet. Not when she had to prove herself worthy to the fae that depended on her success.

Even though Thelia had already defeated Langwidere and Reva was on her way to vanquish Locasta, the biggest threat still remained. If Oz wasn't stopped, none of the other good things mattered. And worse, he would find a way to get rid of Thelia and Reva to keep his throne.

Ozma couldn't let that happen. She needed to cross the desert to see if Mombi was still in her hut. Her heart thump-thumped with the name Jack over and over. What had Mombi told him? That she gave her away? That Tip broke through the magical barrier and made a run for it? Did he think she was dead? But he would never trust whatever lies Mombi had told him. She believed that down to her bones.

Every night in the dark place, for the past two years, she'd thought about him, wanted to see his lovely face, feel his calloused hands against her naked body, his strong hugs that could always calm her fears.

While Reva would try endlessly to forget Crow, Ozma had never once wanted to forget her Jack. Not the orange of his hair under the morning sun, the light sprinkle of freckles on his nose—like flickering stars in a night sky—his high cheekbones, the plumpness of his lips. His *kisses.*

She. Loved. Him. And he loved her. Only, she hadn't been Ozma then when he'd spoken those words to her in his bed, in the lake, beneath the night sky, as the sun rose. She'd been Tippertarius and had been unknowingly forced to live in a male's body. At times, she still yearned to be Tip, but only because he was who Jack had wanted. Not who she wanted to be. If she had a chance to be a male again, it wouldn't feel right.

When she found out she was Ozma, after falling into the dark place, it took some time to get used to, but also felt like she was always meant to be this fae. She was a female, one destined to rule the entirety of Oz. On the day Ozma had broken her unknown curse, she finally felt true to herself. Being a queen was another matter—she didn't truly know if she could succeed at it.

Ozma tried to shove away her too-many thoughts as she squeezed through branches covered in thick moss and stepped over patches of polka-dotted mushrooms and flowered shrubbery. A few birds flew from the trees, pumping their… *Wings.* She'd only had strong, feathery wings for moments, but she knew with her whole heart that she needed them back. They were a part of her, and Mombi had burned them to ash. But once the silver slippers were on her feet, it was possible they would grow once more.

A sparkling river came into view and Ozma stopped at the water and gathered the cool liquid in her canteen. The internal map told her she'd be at the Shifting Sands soon. Even though Mombi's pumpkin patch hadn't been far from it, the Sands had never been possible for Ozma to see because of the barrier, but Jack had told her about its bright multi-colored grains. Still, she had never wanted to cross its sandy peaks. Not after the stories Mombi had told her about creatures emerging from its depths, biting the heads off fae and eating them from the inside out.

As Ozma brought one last handful of water to her lips, the raised scar on her back throbbed. The phantom pain of her wings was always a reminder of Mombi. After stewing so long in the dark place, Ozma was sure she would have the strength to outwit the witch who'd ruined her life. Only one good thing had come from Mombi keeping Ozma from her destiny, and that was Jack. But he'd been stolen away from his family, just as she had.

Determined, she placed her satchel's strap over her head and thought of him as she wandered through the forest toward the desert.

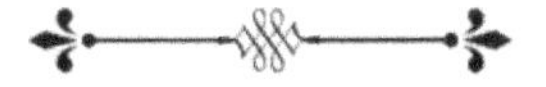

Ozma pressed her fingers to her lips as she stared out at the Shifting Sands. The color was so intense, it made it hard to keep her eyes open. There were so many hues, from dark blues to light purples and bright pinks. It seemed to sway, rhythmically, creating a dance of colors. The light breeze floating across the mounds seemed to sing as if luring its prey.

She shivered at the sight, even though she didn't want to be afraid. All she had to do was get to the other side. The distance across wasn't far, but width wise, it stretched on and on.

She wiggled her toes in the grass, the blades tickling her skin. The Sands could make her see things if it wished, make her *feel* them. Ozma always thought Mombi had lied, but once she'd fallen into the dark place, after swapping her shredded clothing for a blue dress off the skeleton of a dead fae, Reva had told her that the story was true. Each Sand territory had its own hidden dangers. Thankfully, she wouldn't have to cross the Deadly Desert, because she didn't know if being the true queen of Oz would keep her from turning to sand.

"Let's do this, Ozma. Let's go to Jack. He's your home." Blowing out a breath and squaring her shoulders, Ozma pressed one bare foot onto the warm sand. She expected the touch to burn her heel, but instead, it was a light caress. She knew not to trust it. Whichever way the Wizard had crossed, whether the Shifting Sands, the Impassible Desert, the Great Sandy Waste, or even the Deadly Desert, he had to have used the silver slippers or Mombi's help to do it. Otherwise, his mortality would have prevented him from surviving the trip.

Ozma would get the slippers from him, and she would only ever use them for good—if she decided to use them at all after her world was safe.

The winds kicked up, swirling around her, faster and faster. She kept focused, trudging ahead, the grains stinging her eyes and scratching her skin. Beneath her feet, the sand shifted, making it seem like she was walking on water. Ozma knew it wasn't the sand moving on its own, but what lay hidden beneath. *Please stay below until I finish crossing.*

A roaring sounded in the distance, muffled by the sand. If

she sprinted, the creatures below might notice her sooner and chew her to pieces. The sand quaked. The world rumbled. In front of her, a head shot up from the grains. Large black wings flapped. Thick yellow saliva dripped from sharp teeth set in a wide mouth, and thorn-like spikes ran from the top of its head down its massive, blue-scaled body. It wouldn't be the short, clawed arms that grabbed her, but the mouth. And she bet it would be quick.

Ozma's heart seemed to skip a few beats as her body trembled. If only she had her wings, then she could have easily avoided this situation. She genuinely wanted to keep her head attached to her body. All she had was a dagger at her waist that wouldn't do much damage if she used it.

She caught the look in the beast's eyes and jolted out of the way just as the creature's teeth tore into the sand with an ear-piercing shriek. There was no hesitation from her—she sprinted. Pumping her legs as fast as she could, Ozma thought of Jack's face, his eyes, his lips, him pulling her across the sand, though it was really only her who was doing this. On her own.

With a quick glance over her shoulder, she watched as the spiked tail of the beast swished in the air while the rest of the body vanished into the sand.

The edge of the desert wasn't far now. A few moments and she would be safe, but the beast shot up again. Followed by a second. Both studied her with predatory skill, then scrutinized each other, as if neither wanted to share. One dove, mouth wide open, sharp teeth glistening, aiming for the other's throat with a loud growl. A wailing screech echoed.

Ozma suppressed a shudder at the thought of them deciding to divide her and ripping her in half. She took the chance to run again while they were distracted. The heat of the sun beat at her skin as she held her breath, and she didn't breathe again until her feet met grass.

Dropping to her knees, chest heaving, she hurried to turn around. In the small stretch of sand, the two beasts were still fighting, bright red blood pouring from deep wounds on both their bodies. One of the blue creatures buried its fangs into the other, spraying more crimson. The beast unlatched its mouth and let the second creature collapse to the sand, unmoving.

There was victory in the beast's flaming-orange eyes until it spotted Ozma across the barrier of the Sands, safe. A heavy roar escaped the creature's mouth as it dove back into the sand, taking the dead beast with it.

She was so close to where she needed to be, so close to Jack.

Ozma rose from the ground. The tall trees surrounding her were drawn so tightly together that she couldn't glimpse anything through the red flowers growing along the branches.

She pushed a limb out of the way, then another and another until she came across her first sign of life in Loland. Faeries with clear glittery wings sang and danced in the leaves above. Ozma smiled as she watched. The joy that radiated from them would soon spread through Oz. It would take time, and fae would need to rebuild, but the happiness would come. Ozma had experienced her share of darkness—as had Reva, Crow, Tin, and Thelia. But each of them still held hope, and she prayed others would too.

The farther she got through the trees, her heart raced more. Decaying logs full of holes were sprawled across the ground and she hopped over each one, pep blooming with each step. Her smile didn't drop, not once.

A sprinkle of orange peeked through the trees and her smile grew wider. Hot tears streamed down her cheeks and she let out a giggle.

But then her laughter caught in her throat, the smile dropping from her face when there was no flicker of blue where the barrier should have been—it was *gone*. Mombi had never once let the barrier drop. Even the pumpkins seemed to be sparser than they had in the past.

Focus, Ozma.

Something was wrong, and she needed to not worry about

getting to Jack first—she had to see if Mombi was still in her hut. Revenge on the witch would have to take priority, unless she wasn't at the patch.

Her gaze settled on Mombi's light brown home resting in the distance. Mombi's and Jack's huts both appeared the same, as though they remained occupied. The clay pots were still on Jack's porch, the plants in full bloom with blue and purple hyacinths, like always. And Mombi's rocker continued to rest beside her door with her favorite blanket thrown over its back. She hesitated for a moment to go farther, then shoved the nervousness away.

From her waist, Ozma drew out her dagger. Part one of her plan would be to kill Mombi. Part two would be to find Jack. And part three would be to kill the Wizard.

Ozma hovered along the edge of the forest, behind the row of trunks, even though she wanted to run through the field. She doubted Mombi was looking out a window, waiting for Ozma to approach, but she needed to sneak up on her for this to go smoothly.

When she reached the hut, Ozma slipped out from the trees. Mombi didn't keep a single flower around her home. The beds in front of the hut were nothing but dirt gardens with weeds as they had been before. It fit Mombi's personality quite well.

The porch was bare except for the single wooden rocker where Mombi used to sit and watch them work the fields. In that moment, Ozma could hear Mombi screeching at them to work faster and she shoved that aggravating voice away.

Ozma crept in front of the grime-streaked door and pushed open the entrance as quietly as possible, but a teeny squeak sounded and she froze. Gripping the dagger, Ozma stepped inside—the house still smelled of Mombi: nutmeg, ginger, and rotten eggs. The sitting room appeared unchanged, with a canary-yellow settee and a table covered in empty glass bottles and vials that Mombi would use to store antidotes for the Wizard.

Ozma's door was open and she could see that nothing of hers remained. Her wool jacket no longer hung on the wall, her wardrobe of clothing was gone, and the blanket from her bed was now used as a curtain over the far window. It was as if she'd never lived there. But that didn't surprise her.

Slowly, she went toward Mombi's room, her door shut, always protected from anyone going inside. Only, like the barrier around the patch, there was no flicker of blue around it. The barrier had vanished here too. Her lungs stilled as her eyes widened. Something was wrong—Mombi would never leave her room unprotected.

Ozma took a deep swallow, turned the knob, and cracked the door open, a light creak sounding. Her eyes remained widened as she inhaled a mixture of the witch's scent, faerie fruit innards, and lavender. She'd never seen Mombi's room before because of the spells that had been placed around it.

The space was filled with stack after stack of books, several with loose sheaves of paper sticking out. Spellbooks. Besides those, there was only Mombi's bed with rumpled sheets, a wardrobe, and several silver pails for her mixtures.

Jack. What if he wasn't at the patch either? What if he'd gone somewhere else? What if she could never find him again?

The map in her veins could lead her to places, but that was all—she'd tried to feel him before and she couldn't, just as she wouldn't be able to locate Reva. A wounded sound escaped her as she closed the door and rushed from the room, tearing her way out of the hut, back into the heat of the day.

Leaping off the porch, she rushed toward the gray hut on the other side of the patch. Thick, curled vines from the pumpkins struck her legs as she hurried, and she ignored the slight stings at her ankles.

Ozma came to a stop at the edge of the patch, her face hot, catching her breath before she took a step onto the uneven porch. The hyacinths caught her attention again—he had to still be there.

Hand shaking, she gently opened the door in case Mombi was here. The witch had never set foot in Jack's hut, but things seemed to have changed over the last two years and she needed to remain cautious. She gripped the dagger in her hand as she entered the tiny sitting room. The settee and small kitchen table were still in the space, but it sat empty. Paintings hung on the walls that were hers and Jack's, of places they'd wanted to go and visit one day. They weren't very good, but they were theirs. She couldn't help but smile because he'd kept them.

A stirring came from the only other room in the hut, followed by muffled noises. Clenching her blade tighter, Ozma tiptoed down the tiny hallway to the open door.

She furrowed her brow and stopped in the doorway, peering inside. Orange hair, brighter than the pumpkins outside, stood out like a beacon in the room. Her heart rose with elation just as fast as it dropped to ruination the moment that she stepped inside. She couldn't comprehend what she was seeing. Jack's naked body was atop another male with dark hair. And he was thrusting inside him.

With a sharp inhale, Ozma covered her mouth, the dagger dropping from her hand with a loud clang. She backed into the door frame instead of out of the room, making more sound than she'd wanted to. Deep down, Ozma should have known that Jack wouldn't wait for her. She didn't know what Mombi had told him, but she should have known either way.

Jack's head angled over his shoulder from the commotion, his body stilling as his hazel eyes met hers. "Who the fuck are you?"

Tip. Tip. Tip. Ozma just stood there, body trembling. She couldn't look at the male beneath him, only Jack, but anything she wanted to say was lodged in her throat. *Just say who you are.* "Tip's sister," she finally stuttered. And with those words, not waiting for him to respond, she whirled around and took off for the front door.

Her heart pounded with too many emotions as she fled out

of the house and over the pumpkins. A large vine snagged her by the leg, tripping her, and ensnaring her there. Tears rushed down her cheeks while she tugged at the vine.

This was not home. Jack wasn't her home any longer.

Chapter Four

Jack

Market day had been a success. All of the ripest pumpkins sold—for far less than Mombi would've accepted but fuck her—and Jack had traded forgotten potions from Mombi's hut for a new handcart. Once the rest of the crop matured and Jack sold everything on the farm, he would leave. Find his own place in the world and start anew. The Enchanted Isle of Yew, perhaps, or the Isle of Mifkets. He and Tip had dreamed of traveling to both, and he would love to live by the sea.

But those plans had to wait another week, until he had enough coin.

It was an amazing feeling that the coins in his pocket were all his. He didn't have to sneak a few out to pay for a tumble because the scraggly old hag had been gone for a fortnight now. *Bless whatever happened to bring the barrier down.* It had to be related to how weak Mombi had become lately, but he didn't give a damn. This little taste of freedom was only a drop in the bucket. After buying a celebratory *real* bottle of ale—none of that homemade pumpkin shit—there was only one thing missing before he left town.

A body to warm his bed. And he knew just the one.

"Elidyr," he greeted as he approached the male leaning against the corner of a pub. A hanging lamp swung lightly over his head with the gentle night breeze. The elf was shorter than him and taller than Tip, but height didn't matter when he was pressed into a bed. The dark hair and blue eyes were what made this particular prostitute a favorite.

Elidyr smiled coyly and played with the ties holding Jack's shirt closed. "Hello, Jack. It's been a while."

Jack shrugged. "You've been busy."

"Aye." Elidyr's smile widened. "I have. Some trooping faeries passed through and decided to continue their revelry here for a few days."

"Who could blame them?" Jack closed the distance between them and lifted Elidyr's chin. "With a face like this."

Elidyr lightly ran his fingertips up Jack's torso and slid inside the loose ties crossing over his chest. The skin-to-skin contact made him shiver. He wanted more. Needed it. He leaned in and flicked his tongue over Elidyr's bottom lip. The male's fingers curled into his shirt in response.

"I want you for the entire night," Jack breathed. What did he care if it cost more than he could truly afford? He meant to save as much as he could, but desperation clawed at his chest, erasing all reason. A quick fuck in the back alley wouldn't cut it this time. He wanted someone to sleep beside him all night, and be there when he woke in the morning, just so he could pretend he wasn't completely unloved. "I can pay."

"A whole night is expensive," Elidyr said.

"I can pay," Jack repeated and held the bottle of ale up between them. "Help me celebrate."

Elidyr's brow lifted. "Celebrate what?"

"Freedom." Jack tugged at Elidyr's waistband. "Come home with me and I'll pay extra if you wake me up with your mouth."

Elidyr reached up and rapped on the window behind him. "I've got a client for the night."

A portly redcap flung open the window and stuck her head out. "Ah, Jack!" The madam's pleasant expression turned to a scowl. "You can afford an entire night? What will Mombi say? Elidyr is one of my best males and I can't have him injured."

"Mombi's gone." He dug into his pocket and tossed her a silver coin. "Half now. Half when he leaves in the morning."

The redcap caught it midair, bit the coin, and nodded. "Where is Mombi then?"

"Damned if I know," he said with a shrug. After fourteen days, he hoped she was dead.

The redcap licked her lips and stared at him as if trying to detect a lie. Finally, she waved them off with a quick, "have fun."

Oh, we'll have fun. Jack's cock stiffened slightly at the thought of Elidyr's lips wrapped around his length. *All night.*

"Lead the way," Elidyr said with a playful grin.

Jack turned on his heel and started out of town with Elidyr trailing behind him. His heart thumped wildly at the promise of pleasure, but it was tainted by something darker—longing. For Elidyr to be Tip. For someone to tell Jack it was all a lie. That Tip had never left him and was alive somewhere. Waiting for him. Wanting him as badly as Elidyr wanted his money. That Tip needed him with every bone in his body.

But no one could tell Jack those things.

Because Tip didn't choose him. Tip chose to abandon him to a life enslaved to Mombi, so fucking someone who closely resembled his ex-lover would *not* make him feel like he was betraying their relationship. He would *not* feel guilty.

Not even a little.

Jack woke the next afternoon to Elidyr's wet tongue gliding up his swollen cock. His lips twitched and a moan slipped from his throat. Opening his eyes was out of the question, at least for the moment. He could pretend better if he didn't see. Pretend that the breath skating over his glistening head came from a different male. Pretend that, if he *did* open his eyes, he would see the brightest blue ones looking up at him.

"Morning," Elidyr said with a sleep-filled voice far too deep to belong to Tip. "Or perhaps more like afternoon."

The image of his ex-lover vanished from behind Jack's eyelids. It wasn't Tip—it was a fae he *paid* to show him attention. The realization of what he'd done, how low he'd fallen, always struck the hardest when he first woke. Before the ale could drown out the humiliation. *No.* He would. Not. Feel. Guilty. If Tip loved him, he wouldn't have left. There was no reason Jack shouldn't enjoy himself. No reason not to seek momentary pleasure.

He sprung from the bed with a frustrated growl and jerked his chin to the headboard. "Hold onto that."

Elidyr inched up the bed, his dark hair rumpled, and bent over to hold onto the wooden frame. Jack took in Elidyr's lean form and pale skin. He hadn't noticed just how pale he was in the shadowy alleys where they fucked, but the sunlight made it painfully obvious. Tip's skin was darker from working in the field all day. Golden and beautiful.

Just close your eyes, he told himself as he knelt behind the fae and gripped his ass. Elidyr pressed back into his touch. Jack fisted his own cock, pumping until it was completely hard, and grabbed the oil from the bedside table.

Elidyr moaned the moment Jack slid inside him. The sound rang false to his ears, but he would ignore that too. Ignore, ignore, ignore. And simply *feel.* Feel each thrust. Thrust after thrust after—

A loud clang sounded behind him, followed by the shuffle of feet and a softer thud. Jack froze and his eyes flew open. Over his shoulder stood a young female in a blue dress. Blonde hair, blue eyes. *Gorgeous.* But no one came here. Ever. Unless she was new to the brothel and came to collect Elidyr on behalf of the redcap.

"Who the fuck are you?" he demanded.

She stared at him with a pained expression before blurting, "Tip's sister." Then she whirled around and fled the hut.

Tip's sister? Tip's *sister*? Her words immediately made him go limp. He pulled out of Elidyr and scoured the floor for his pants. There was never any mention of a sister or any other family for that matter. Not from Tip. Not from Mombi. "Shit," he muttered.

"Here." Elidyr lifted his eyebrows and threw Jack's pants across the room. "Your lover?"

"Not even close," he said, panting, as he tried desperately to get his legs in his pants. Why was one leg inside out? "Damn it!" His hands shook as he fixed the fabric, his pulse echoing in his ears. "You should leave."

Elidyr began collecting his own clothes. "The other half of my money?"

He shoved a hand in his pocket and tossed him a coin. Without bothering to buckle his pants, Jack raced out the open door. The female was halfway across the pumpkin patch, sprawled in the dirt with her foot caught in the vines.

Jack sprinted after her, leaping over rows of pumpkins, while holding his waistband in place. The female saw him coming and scrambled to her feet.

"Wait!" he called. But she was already bolting straight for Mombi's hut. Jack pushed himself faster until he was close enough to grab her wrist. "Please wait."

"Let go of me," she cried.

"Okay," Jack agreed slowly. She couldn't simply show up, claim to be Tip's sister, and disappear. He needed answers first. "But … wait. Okay?"

"Fine," she grumbled and Jack released her.

For a moment, they faced each other, steadying their rapid breaths, before Jack asked, "You're Tip's sister?"

"I…" She swallowed hard. "I'm Ozma."

"Ozma." Jack looked her up and down. She looked nothing

like Tip. They had the same vivid blue eyes but that was where the resemblance ended. Where his hair was nearly black, hers was so blonde that it could've been spun from sunlight. She was taller than Tip, too. Her features were delicate, her lips full, where Tip's cheekbones and jaw had been sharp-edged, his lips wide. "I'm Jack."

"I know," she whispered.

Jack cocked his head and ran his free hand through his hair. "Sorry about back at the hut. I wasn't expecting company."

"Of course not," she said in a harsh voice.

At a loss for words, Jack simply stared at Ozma. A sister… Tip had a sister. But how did she find this place? And why did she come now? Was it Mombi's doing? Had she sent this female to taunt him? Or check on him, perhaps? What kind of game was this?

He was torn between being patient and shaking the answers from Ozma. But mostly, he wanted to hide in his hut so she wouldn't see his shame. The first time he'd brought someone back home, fucked someone other than Tip in his bed, and Ozma caught him. Of all the fae… He quickly buckled his pants.

"You should get back to your lover," she snapped.

"He's not my lover." When Ozma glared at him, he added, "Not in the way you're thinking."

"Sure," Ozma mumbled, barely loud enough for him to hear.

His breath caught. "What's that supposed to mean?"

"Nothing." Ozma's voice crackled with emotion. "I'm just here for Tip's things."

"Tip didn't *have* things," Jack growled. A few changes of clothes and essential items, but nothing more. Especially not two years later. *Patience.* Scaring her away wouldn't get him the answers he needed. "Did Mombi send you? Are you going to report back to her? Tell her that I brought someone here?"

Ozma's eyes widened. "Why would I need to report to Mombi when she can see you for herself?"

Did she really not know Mombi had left? Could she be who

she said she was? His gaze fell to the ground as he ran different explanations through his mind, and Ozma's bare feet caught his attention. "Tip never wore shoes either," he blurted before he could stop himself.

Ozma huffed and turned toward Mombi's hut again, then ran.

Jack stayed where he was and watched her go. There was a familiarity about Ozma. Not her blossom aroma, but beneath that lingered sugar and crisp autumn leaves, just as it had with Tip. And there'd been something in her eyes… It was like she *knew* him. Like she was personally offended by what she had walked in on.

Had Tip survived the Shifting Sands? Had he found his sister and told her about their relationship? Had they laughed at the idea of him alone with Mombi? No… Even if Tip didn't love him, he wasn't *that* cruel. Perhaps Tip sent Ozma here so he wouldn't have to see Mombi again? Or so he wouldn't have to face Jack? Jack looked up just as Ozma disappeared into Mombi's hut and felt the cracks in his heart breaking open again.

Chapter Five

Ozma

Jack had run after Ozma. But of course he did—a strange female barged straight into his hut while he was... She shook her head, trying to escape the vision of Jack with the other male. *What was I thinking, telling Jack I was Tip's sister?*

She wanted to leave, should leave, but she couldn't. Instead, she ran toward Mombi's because that was the only place where she could lock herself in for the moment. Ozma was the true queen of Oz and she shouldn't be wasting time hiding in another dark place to cry. However, she needed to regain focus. This was all Mombi's and the Wizard's fault and, more than ever, she needed to run a blade across their throats. For making her feel this way, for making Jack so easily turn to a new lover. Perhaps Jack didn't love her as much as he'd claimed.

A small voice rang in Ozma's head, whispering to her that Jack likely believed Tip was dead. She batted at her ear—the voice of reason—as she sprinted, leaping over pumpkins. It didn't matter because she'd *seen him* mounting another and she couldn't unsee that.

Ozma knew she was being deceitful, but if she did tell him

the truth, it would always be Tip, Tip, Tip. Jack might not say the words aloud but he would compare her to Tip, to who she used to be. But she wasn't that fae anymore, in body or mind. From being in that dark place with Reva, learning things, discovering the world—even though she'd yet to see it in its entirety. Stars above, she couldn't stop seeing Jack *thrusting* inside that other male.

With shaking hands, Ozma threw open the entrance to Mombi's and rushed inside. The door slammed, echoing within the hut, rattling the walls as she bolted the lock. She didn't want to be back in this place. This hut. This *patch.* Earlier, she'd been so focused on having her blissful reunion with Jack after murdering Mombi, to be overly bothered by being here, but neither had happened. Too much time had passed for Jack.

Standing alone, in the middle of this familiar room, seeing the glass vials, the switches in the corner that Mombi would use to slap Ozma's knuckles, she shivered. Ozma could feel the stings now, along with the painfully vicious strikes against her cheek. No, *Tip's* knuckles, his cheek. Her body trembled—it was too much. She didn't miss being in male form, especially now with the memories resurfacing.

Ozma cupped her nose and mouth, to stifle any more crying. As her chest heaved, she dreamed of shattering Mombi's glass vials to pieces, setting fire to the hut. Not now, though. She only had the strength to release an ear-shattering scream. What could Mombi do if Ozma did destroy her things? What could be worse than what she'd already done? Put Ozma back in the dark place? Kill her? Make her forget? Perhaps that would be better than the betrayal and hurt consuming her at that moment.

A tapping came at the door and Ozma froze, knowing it wouldn't be Mombi because she wouldn't knock at her own hut. Why couldn't he just leave her alone? But she knew why… Ozma should have just told him she was someone else. *Anyone* else.

She didn't want to see him. She did want to see him. No. She *did not* want to see him.

The knob turned and the door rattled as Jack tried to open it, insistent, urgent, like the frantic beat of her heart.

Taking a deep breath, she went to the door and unbolted it before yanking it open. "Yes?" she asked, voice soft, too soft. Ozma should have snapped, asked him why he'd been tumbling another. It had been two years, but Jack *knew* Mombi, and he shouldn't have believed anything she'd said.

Jack ran a hand through his hair, grabbing at the short curls before a lock fell right at his brow. He stared at her, throat bobbing, his eyes dancing with an uncertain emotion. "I wanted to give you a moment to yourself, but you can't stay at Mombi's."

Ozma opened her mouth to say she needed more than a moment when he pressed a finger against her lips. To shush her. She narrowed her eyes, clenching her teeth, but her heart kicked up at his touch anyway. Until a familiar scent of oil hit her nose and she took a step back, away from him. That single digit that had touched her body everywhere … but not *this* body. He'd been with another male only minutes ago.

"Now," Jack continued, dropping his hand and licking his lower lip, "we're going to have a little chat. You're going to tell me why you're here, *how* you're here, and if Mombi truly didn't send you. I want the truth."

The truth… He wanted the *truth*. Before, she would have told him, she would have confided everything to him, but after seeing what she had, she just couldn't find the words.

"I'm not working for Mombi," Ozma whispered. She straightened so she was closer to his height and lifted her chin. It was strange to now see him almost eye to eye instead of having to look farther up at him. "I came here to kill her, not to collect Tip's things. And yes, I'm Tip's sister. Whether you want to believe it or not is up to you, but I am." And in a way, she believed her words. She'd been Tip in the past, but it felt like another fae now, one she didn't want to go back to. Perhaps Jack was just part of that old world, that broken place. Perhaps Jack was her lover then, but not meant to be hers now.

Jack cocked his head and crossed his arms as he leaned against the doorframe. "You being his sister doesn't make a damn bit of sense. Tip died while crossing the Shifting Sands so there's no way you could've known Mombi held him captive once." He paused, a glimmer of hope crossing his face. "Or are you telling me he's still alive? Is that how you knew to come here?"

That was what Jack was hoping for. To have Tip back. Because he believed that, maybe, Mombi had lied to him, that Tip was still out there alive somewhere. Tip was Ozma so it was true... She almost told him in that moment. Almost. *But* if he'd believed there was a chance Tip could be alive, then why was he taking a lover to his bed—the bed where Tip and Jack had been together, time after time—instead of searching for him. The barrier was gone so there was no excuse.

"Mombi didn't lie to you about that," Ozma finally said. "Tip is dead, but it was she who killed him."

Jack pushed off the doorframe, his shoulders dropping as he inched close, closer. She couldn't tell if he believed her. "Then tell me, pretty blossom, how do you know all this?"

She could give him a partial truth. "Because … because Mombi stole me too." Her eyes focused on the spot where she'd become Ozma: across from the decaying wooden chair, where a large oval mirror hung on the wall. She locked her gaze on her own image. "Only, I was held in the mirror here all this time." She pointed to the glass. "Tip had an argument with Mombi and his magic somehow came to life, but before he could use it, she turned him into ash. So, Tip may not have known about me, but I knew everything. After Tip died, Mombi sent me somewhere else, a dark place, and before you ask how I got out, it was because Dorothy returned." She paused, tears pricking at her eyes. "So that's why I'm here, to murder Mombi for what she's done, to Tip, and to me."

Jack took a step back, rubbing a hand over his mouth and jaw. "I don't know what to say. Mombi isn't here—she left when she heard Dorothy had returned."

Ozma's eyes widened. "She knows?" Of course she would. Word must have spread like wildfire when Thelia came back to Oz. This wasn't good. Ozma hadn't known who Dorothy was when she'd lived in Loland, but she'd learned all about her in the dark place from Reva. "What happened to the barrier?"

"I don't know. It vanished a few minutes after the bitch left to go to the Wizard."

Perhaps the witch was growing weaker. Why would Jack stay if he wasn't trapped inside? But she didn't ask him. "Has the Wizard been here recently?"

He shook his head. "I haven't seen him in years and don't know where he is."

"I'll have to find Mombi then."

Jack arched a brow, scanning her up and down. "Show me your magic."

"What?" She wrinkled her nose, confused by his sudden change of mood and question.

"Show me"—he stepped forward, lifted a lock of her hair, twirling it around his finger—"how you're going to defeat Mombi. Because if you've watched her from that mirror most of your life, then you'll know you need to have a pretty damn good amount of magic."

She closed one eye, squinted the other, and cringed. "Um, I don't have any at the moment."

"Let me understand this." Jack dropped his hand from her hair and shook his head. "You have zero magic and think you can defeat one of the most powerful witches in Oz?"

"Listen," Ozma said, determined. "I have a blade and I've learned how to be sneaky, how to kill someone." She thought about the Wheeler she'd stabbed through the heart after Reva had struck the rest of the clan dead with her magic. "It wouldn't be that difficult if I were fast, if Mombi was unaware."

Jack stared at her for a long moment, studying her face. "I see that hate burning in your eyes, the way it did in Tip's, the way it does in mine. And I believe you really are Tip's sister, only because you have the same eyes as him. I would recognize that bright blue anywhere. But, if he were still here, and he knew about you, he wouldn't want you to do this."

Before she could reply, Jack scooped her off the floor, making her gasp. He cradled her in his arms as he strode out of the hut, closing the door with his boot.

"What are you doing?" she screeched when she finally found words.

"You're coming to my place for the night," he replied with an easy shrug.

"I will not!" She tried to wriggle from his hold. "Not with a … lover there."

"He left, so it's just you and me." Jack stepped over several pumpkins as he walked in the direction of his hut. "If you promise not to run again, I'll set you down, though."

"Fine." She honestly just needed to go somewhere and rest. The day was catching up to her. Not only the day, but the past two years of constantly being on the move and trying not to be killed. Now that she was at the patch, she could relax for a moment, even if nothing was ending up as she'd planned.

Jack lowered her to the ground and she walked beside him, leaving a two-person gap between them until they reached his hut.

Her lids fluttered, the exhaustion washing over her, as she peered at him in front of the door.

He stared at her, a line settling between his brows like he wanted to ask more questions, but he didn't. "Go inside and get some rest. I have a few things to take care of before heading to the market tomorrow. By the looks of things, you'll get to join me."

Ozma didn't have the energy to argue as she nodded and stepped into Jack's hut. She didn't focus on anything around her, just went to his room and scooped up the dagger she'd dropped earlier. She set it on top of his dresser beside an unlit lantern.

Even though she wanted to collapse on the bed, she just couldn't. Not after Jack… She sank to the hard floor, curled her knees to her chest, and imagined she was in the same place, but back in time with Jack.

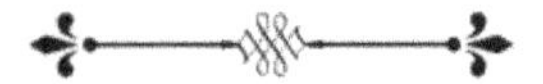

Ozma opened her eyes, surrounded by darkness and shadows swaying across from her. She jolted up with a gasp, her gaze settling on a flickering lantern. For a moment, she thought she was back in the dark place with Reva. But then she recognized the rafters of the ceiling and ugly frayed curtains. She was in Jack's hut.

How long had she slept?

She stood from the floor and stretched her spine. In front of the lantern, beside her dagger, was a bowl full of fruit. Jack had left this? Turning, she searched the bedroom for him, but he wasn't there.

Tiptoeing to the door, she peered out through the narrow crack. Light snoring came from the sitting room, signaling Jack was there and asleep.

Now that Ozma was rested, her head clear, she remembered Mombi's room, the stacks of books. There had to be something inside them—a location spell, one she could use to track down the witch.

Ozma tucked her dagger at her hip, then collected a piece of fruit and the lantern before going to the window. Little by little, she lifted the glass, each push releasing a soft creak. As Tip, she'd snuck out of this window too many times to count, so Mombi wouldn't catch her leaving out the front door.

Outside, all was quiet, except for the flutter of faerie wings somewhere in the forest. The barrier had been out past the trees and around the lake, but not even the small faeries could slip past Mombi's magic. She wondered if they tried to now or if they assumed the barrier was still in place.

Trudging quietly across the patch, she bit into the sweet fruit and attempted not to let herself think of Jack. Only focus on the next step, which was finding Mombi.

The hut stood quiet and dark as she opened the door. An eerie feeling poured over her as she stepped inside. Darkness always made things worse. Ozma's hands trembled as she thought about trees from the dark place reaching out with thorned limbs.

The sweet, rotten scent assaulted her as she entered Mombi's room. Holding the lantern higher, she surveyed the space and the messy stacks of books.

There had to be something here she could use. Ozma lit the candles along the wall with the flame of her lantern, giving herself more light. She picked a book up and thumbed through its yellowed pages, the drawings of mutilated bodies, blood spilling from fae babies' mouths. The things Mombi had done in the past with these spells churned her stomach.

After finding nothing useful, she searched another and another. Most were spells that involved conjuring up the dead or opening doors to dark worlds.

There had to be a location spell somewhere. Mombi always had an alternate plan and letting Jack go to town—even compelled—was a risk. The witch would want to track him down if he never came back. She closed her eyes, the map of Oz lighting up within her, hoping that she could possibly find Mombi this time. But she couldn't, nothing had changed.

Her hand halted when she discovered, not what she was looking for, but something else, circled in what appeared to be faded blood. A curse to take away a fae's true identity, which would allow them to have their magic hidden too. As she turned the page, a withering folded note, tucked inside, caught her attention. She opened it and read:

Steal the child growing in Lurline's belly.
Use magic to alter the child's identity.

Find silver slippers to draw magic from the child.
Create immortality.

Ozma placed the note in the book and slammed it shut. That must be why Mombi had changed her instead of killing her. The Wizard… The shoes had brought him to Mombi's the last time because of the burst of Ozma's magic. She didn't have any now, though… And according to the note, it had to be because the slippers were drawing the magic from her right now, the way they must have been while she was locked away in the dark place.

Chest heaving, she put aside what she'd uncovered about herself for now. Because it didn't matter in that moment. Finding Mombi did. After going through several more books involving hearts of sprites, heads of gnomes, fingers and eyes of fauns, she came across something that could potentially work. All she would need to do was create a concoction with a piece of skin from herself and something personal from the other fae, along with a few other things that Mombi would already have there. Then chant the spell words and she would be able to follow a magic trail to her target that only she could see.

This is it. She grinned as she tore the pages from the book and placed them in her satchel for safekeeping. Tomorrow she would come back and create the mixture.

Ozma left the house and glanced at Jack's. Her chest tightened, and she realized she didn't want to go back there for the remainder of the night. She wanted to bathe from her long journey, then she would sleep beside the lake until morning.

While staring up at the night sky, Ozma studied the full moon, and made a wish for Reva and Crow, then Tin and Thelia. For their safety.

Pushing past several trees, she slipped into the forest. The crooked limbs seemed to stretch up to the stars as she walked around the group of small boulders and stopped in front of the lake. The moon reflected off the glassy surface while the liquid rippled. Setting down the lantern in a patch of grass beside the log that was hers and Jack's, Ozma removed her satchel, the rope across her waist, and dress. She caught a whiff of herself and she nearly choked—bathing was the perfect choice.

As she stepped into the cool water, the liquid swaying against her, Ozma ignored the shiver that rolled through her body. She swam out to the center, practically feeling the grains from the desert wash away. Once she found Mombi, Ozma wondered how exactly she should kill her. The dagger through her heart? Across her throat? Through her eye? Her first kill had been the Wheeler with Reva. Before she'd changed into Ozma, the thought of murder would have terrified her. But Reva had taught her that sometimes it was necessary. To make things better, it was sometimes crucial.

Once she cleaned off well enough, Ozma started to swim back to the edge of the lake when a *click, click* sound erupted from behind one of the trees. She stilled mid-swim, breaths halting, and whirled around in the water. It came again, louder than before. She'd never heard anything like it. The moon gave off light but not enough to illuminate the entire forest. Shadows enfolded around her as the wind blew.

A splash into the water made her suck in a sharp breath. She didn't linger—she swam, faster than she ever had. Behind her, the thing thrashing through the lake drew closer. Two hands grabbed her by the waist, claws digging in, drawing blood. Ozma released a terrified scream as she was yanked beneath the water, her attacker pulling her down, deeper and deeper.

She shoved her elbow back and struck the soft flesh of whatever it was. The claws loosened and Ozma swam rapidly to the surface. Just when she caught a gulp of air, the creature snatched her ankle and hauled her down again. A hand clamped around her mouth, and she bit it, but the creature didn't relent.

Her heart pounded harder, her lungs growing thirstier and thirstier for air. Ozma fought to hold her eyes open, but she couldn't. This wasn't the way she'd ever expected to die, not in this lake that had always been safe. The last thought that came to her was if she could so easily be killed, then perhaps she wasn't a true queen after all.

Chapter Six

Jack

The slide of wood-on-wood woke Jack. He knew exactly what that sound was—*the bedroom window.* He stayed where he was on the worn, tattered rug, feigning sleep. Ozma was sneaking out and he wanted to know why. If Tip's sister was running off to report to Mombi, he needed to know. The floor creaked and the rustle of her skirts filled the air as Ozma slipped through the window.

Jack's pulse raced as he forced himself to continue lying there. *One. Two. Three.* He cracked his eyes open. The moth-eaten curtains were closed so she wouldn't be able to see him moving about. Slowly, he got to his feet and crept into the bedroom. The spot on the floor was vacant where Ozma had been sleeping and the window was, indeed, open. Peeking out into the night, he caught a glimpse of Ozma's golden hair weaving through the pumpkin field toward Mombi's hut.

"What are you doing, Blossom?" he whispered to himself.

He waited until she was halfway to the hut before darting out the window after her—the door would make too much noise. His bare feet landed quietly in the dirt and he slipped through the shadows, watching her sprint. If Ozma wasn't working with Mombi, what did she want so badly inside the hut? And why would she need to sneak away to find it? Sure, there were a lot of things of the witch's that many fae would desire, but some fae were more nefarious than others. He'd been impulsive when he'd scooped her up and brought her home with him, but she'd looked ready to collapse. And perhaps he'd been hoping a good rest would make her more eager to speak to him. He had so many questions—the mirror she lived in, the dark place, who her and Tip's parents were…

Ozma disappeared into Mombi's hut and shut the door behind her. Jack ran as silently as he could, until he reached the witch's hut. He pressed his back to the rotting wood walls and slid closer to the window where a crack marred the glass. Inch by inch he moved, afraid she would spot his bright orange hair. He vaguely regretted not grabbing a shirt to shield against the chilly night.

Too late now.

Jack poked his head up and squinted into the dark hut. A lantern—*his* lantern—illuminated the corner bedroom, followed by the sudden flicker of more candlelight. *Mombi's room, eh?* Suspicious. He hadn't tried to go in there himself after the barrier dropped—hadn't cared to—but he regretted that now. Did Mombi have some sort of communication apparatus in there? Or was Ozma tasked with bringing her forgotten items? He *wanted* to believe she'd been trapped in a mirror but… He let out a quick huff. *But nothing.* Perhaps he only believed Ozma because that meant Tip hadn't left him at all—though it did mean there was no room left to doubt his death. Mombi's tale had always left the smallest crack of hope that it was a lie, that Tip hadn't died, but Ozma's…

Shaking his head, he returned his focus to the flickering light with a growing sense of anxiety. He wished Mombi had a window in her bedroom so he could sneak around back to see what Ozma was doing in there. A shadow moved now and again, and items sailed across the room as she threw them, but Ozma didn't reappear in the main room of the hut for ages. When she did, the candle flames danced across her face. She looked … unnerved. Her features pinched, her bottom lip pressed between her teeth, she studied the hut as if she'd never seen it before. Jack narrowed his eyes. Surely there were some strange things inside Mombi's room, but if Ozma truly had been trapped in the mirror, a witness to everything the witch had done, he doubted a few pickled body parts would upset her.

Shit.

Ozma was heading straight for the door. Jack sprinted around the side of the hut and waited. The door opened and shut. Light fell over the ground, swaying with her steps. *The woods?* Why the fuck would this female go into the woods in the middle of the night? And to be moving so confidently, as if she knew exactly where she was going… How, if she'd been trapped in a mirror, would she know the layout of Mombi's property so well?

Even more suspicious…

A kernel of contempt grew within Jack. Ozma had shown up here … and lied to him. But why? To what end? Her eyes truly were the same unique hue as Tip's, so he believed they were related, but that didn't mean Mombi wasn't controlling her. If that were the case, it wouldn't be as if Ozma wanted to lie to him, only that she had to. Still, it cast the shadow of doubt over everything she'd said. She wanted to kill Mombi, did she? He had always wanted the same thing, yet Mombi was still alive. And not because there hadn't been a single opportunity. Dooming himself to a potential life stuck inside the barrier wasn't on his list of goals. He fisted his hands at his sides.

What the fuck do I do? Who am I supposed to believe?

He'd only ever trusted one fae—Tip. And then he'd either left or been killed. Whatever his fate, it had destroyed a part of Jack. The very small, almost non-existent side of him that had wanted to have faith in others, had been smashed beneath the boot of sorrow.

So he followed Ozma, a shadow among the trees, until she came upon the lake. The moon lit the clearing around the shore where the softest grass grew. A fallen log had been rolled up to the water's edge by Tip long ago and remained there as a bench. They'd spent many hours there, baring their souls, and eventually, their bodies.

And now Ozma was setting her lantern down beside it as if it were the most natural thing in the world. *How did you know the way to this place if you were trapped somewhere else?* Jack took a step forward to demand the answer when her dress fell from her shoulders to pool at her feet. His breath hitched at the sight of her bare ass, the exposed curves, and … was that a scar? A jagged oval marred the center of her back, the healed patch of skin appearing thick and almost glossy. His heart softened slightly at the agony that wound must've caused her.

Ozma flipped her long hair over her shoulders and stepped toward the lake. Jack retreated into the woods far enough so she wouldn't notice him, and so he couldn't be accused of spying on her if he was caught. Not that he wanted to see her naked body—though his cock definitely wanted another peek—but he couldn't let her vanish. Not without figuring out everything she was hiding.

Though clearly a fuckable backside is on that list.

No.

He could *not* lust after Tip's sister. Even a whore like himself needed to have some restraint.

A loud splash sounded from the lake, and Jack leaned against a tree to wait for her to finish bathing. He yanked a red leaf from a low hanging branch and ripped it into tiny little pieces. How should he go about demanding answers? Ozma didn't seem overly excited to share what she already had and would likely give him issues when he tried to fill in the holes.

Fuck this shit.

He would just voice his doubts and wait for the pretty

blossom to reveal the truth. He'd kiss it from her if he had to. Dip his tongue between her lips and taste the flower's nectar. Gently spread apart the petals to see what lay within. His cock stiffened again.

Whoa. Stop it, he chastised himself. *She's Tip's sister and a liar.*

A damned beautiful liar, though.

A scream broke the night air. The hair on Jack's arms stood on end as he bolted toward the lake. There had never been anything nasty living in the water, but Mombi's barrier was down now. Not only could Jack get out, but other creatures could get in.

Jack skidded to a halt in the clearing just in time to see Ozma get completely dragged beneath the dark water. "Oye!" he screamed at … whatever it was. "Don't even fucking think about it!" Before the words finished leaving his mouth, he was knee deep in the lake without realizing he'd moved. "Ozma!"

Shit. Shit shit shit shit shit.

Where was she?

He dove, searching. And searching and searching. All he saw was endless dark water and swaying plant life.

His heartbeat echoed in his ears and his frantic movements kicked up the muck. A scream built in his chest. *Fuck no, you don't!* he thought at whatever had Tip's sister. He needed to save her for Tip's sake. For himself.

He surfaced for a gulp of air and dove again. This time his hand brushed something soft and string-like, and he gripped it. A hard tug came from the other end. *Gotcha.* He used his other hand to grip what had to be Ozma's hair, then worked his way down until he found her head. The fact that she wasn't grabbing for him set his blood pumping faster and faster, but if he could get her to shore, it would be fine.

It had to be fine.

For Tip.

There was no other choice but for her to be okay.

Jack found Ozma's hands, moved his grip up, and hooked

her under her arms. Then he kicked hard for the surface of the lake. A high-pitched screech flowed through the water, echoing down to Jack's bones. He almost released Ozma as his body tried to curl in on itself.

His gaze met a pair of white eyes, within a strangely human face, glowing through the dirt, illuminating the area. *Undine.* A particularly nasty water faerie that could also roam the land in search of a new home. He bared his teeth at the fae and aimed his next kick at her face. The heel of his foot connected with her nose. He felt a satisfying *crunch* and blood further clouded the water around her head.

Jack used the undine's moment of surprise to yank Ozma up, up, up, not stopping until they were both completely on land where the undine wouldn't hunt. He flipped Ozma to her back and started pressing on her bare chest in even compressions.

"Come on, come on," he urged. "Don't die."

As if hearing his desperate words, Ozma coughed. Water spewed from her mouth and she rolled to her side, sputtering. Jack leaned back on his heels, gasping for air along with her, and ran both hands through his wet hair.

"Shit, Blossom," he wheezed. "What were you thinking coming here alone? Anything could be living in there now that the barrier's down." Even though he wouldn't have expected an undine to move in. But this was *his* lake. His and Tip's. He would have to come back later and kill the undine because there was no way he was giving this place up.

She shot him an angry, sideways glance.

"So you *weren't* thinking," he spat.

"Stop. Talking," she said in a hoarse voice and sat up.

Jack unconsciously flicked a glance at her chest and the peaked nipples that greeted him. He hadn't meant to look. It was absolutely inappropriate given the circumstances, but he couldn't stop his eyes from sliding downward.

"Look somewhere else." Ozma quickly crossed her arms over her chest as though she were ashamed of something.

"Sorry! I didn't mean to." He squeezed his eyes shut and willed away the image of her breasts, nipples hard from the cold, before opening them again. "Are you … okay?"

She seemed to think for a moment, a line creasing her brows. "Something grabbed me."

"An undine," Jack supplied. "She must've been searching for a new home and found the lake uninhabited."

Ozma slowly nodded, her teeth chattering.

Jack stood to gather her satchel, dress, and the lantern. "Come on. Let's get you inside so you can warm up."

Ozma eased back to her feet and took the dress from him, pulling it over her sopping wet body. When they returned to his hut, Jack would give her one of his shirts to sleep in so her dress could dry in front of the fireplace.

"You didn't answer my question," he said when they started walking back toward the field. "Are you okay?"

"I think so." She licked her lips. "Thanks for … saving me. How did you know I was there?"

"Of course," he mumbled. "I heard your scream and came." He wouldn't tell her that he'd only been able to do so because he'd followed her. Or that he was more concerned with getting answers about Tip than he was with her personally. Because, though he was a selfish asshole, he couldn't let her know that.

Yet.

Chapter Seven

Ozma

Sunlight spilled through the window, shining in Ozma's left eye, causing her to squint. She'd been staring at the ceiling of Jack's hut for most of the night after he'd patched her up. Then, without her asking, Jack had changed the tumbled sheets of the bed. Ozma still couldn't bring herself to sleep on it, though.

A dull throb pulsed at her waist from where the undine's claws had dug into her flesh, but Jack's healing ointment had done its job.

During the night, she couldn't stop thinking about what would have happened if Jack hadn't come to the lake. Too much of Oz would've been let down because she'd failed before she even started. Each passing day, the weight on her shoulders was growing heavier with the Wizard and Mombi out there, still alive.

Magic would have helped her, but she had to settle for her own smarts, her dagger, and Mombi's spell books.

The door swung open, and she lurched forward to find Jack, head cocked and mouth turned up into a smirk.

"Rise and shine, Blossom," he purred, motioning her forward with a finger. "Come on."

Ozma's heart pounded harder at that voice, his gesture, that new pet name he called her yet again. Then there was him without his shirt on the night before. Each muscle was taut and firm, and she knew it was from the work he did on the farm. She shook the image away and refocused on how he was acting.

"Why?" Ozma asked hesitantly.

"Did you forget we're going to the market today? You get to help me with the pumpkins, and in return, you'll get another meal." Jack tossed her a deep blue fruit and she easily caught it. "Chop, chop! I want to make at least two trips today."

The market. Of course. But part of her interest was extremely piqued by this wild concept. Now she would get to see if it was truly how she'd imagined it. "Let me get dressed first."

His eyes seemed to linger on her, expression unreadable, before shutting the door. The previous night hung between them—him *seeing* her naked body, his gaze resting on her then too. But she hadn't wanted him to see her body for the first time like that, all at once. She glanced down, noticing Jack's tunic. *Is he annoyed that I'm still wearing his shirt?* He'd given it to her when they'd returned to his hut since her dress had been too damp to sleep in.

Making a low groan of frustration, she tugged off his tunic and shimmied back into her dress. She bit into the piece of fruit as she left the hut and walked outside into the patch. The sun lay hidden behind the clouds and the sky was turning a light shade of gray. A gust of wind swished past her, blowing the vines of the pumpkins, near where Jack stood.

Beside him were mostly empty crates and one filled with small pumpkins. On his other side rested a cart on wheels loaded with larger ones. She hadn't missed having to gut the fruit day after day for Mombi's spells and pies.

"I think it might rain," Ozma said, padding up beside him.

"A little water never killed anyone." Jack peered over his shoulder, lifting the crate of fruit. "Can you take that one?" He pointed at the cart, then paused and reached for it. "Never mind.

I don't want you pulling at your wounds."

"I'm fine." She arched a brow and grabbed the wooden handle, tugging the pumpkins forward. They jostled side to side. Her wounds stung for a moment, but she didn't let it show.

Jack wiped the sweat from his brow with the back of his hand and they started walking toward the forest.

Ozma practically held her breath as they skirted around narrow tree trunks where the barrier should've been. And, even though it wasn't there, she still couldn't believe that she was able to go into uncharted territory of Loland.

Once outside the former boundary line, heart still pounding, she took a deep inhale, the woodsy and sweet scent enveloping her. She wondered what the buildings would look like, and what the world outside her entrapment held. And now she would finally know—get to see the places Jack went when he'd been commanded to leave the patch.

Past rocks and boulders, a creek trickled with water. Bushes full of pink and purple berries surrounded the edge of it. The trees seemed to grow wider the farther they got. A tiny brown and green rose goblin covered in thorns leapt out from a crooked hole in a tree, baring its teeth.

Jack hissed back. The rose goblin yelped and tucked its head back inside. Ozma couldn't control her chuckle.

"So," Jack drawled. "Tell me about this dark place you were at…"

He was digging for information from her because he still didn't trust her. Nobody else would be able to tell, but she could. Ozma needed to avoid his suspicion until she could make the potion at Mombi's.

"After Mombi removed me from the mirror and banished me from Oz, I fell into a place with darkness all around. There were things down there that made it so you wouldn't want to sleep. I was constantly on the move, fleeing from beasts that could rip you apart in one bite, and trees that could tear you in half. But I wasn't alone—that's where I met Dorothy's mother,

Reva." They'd never seen another living soul there other than the beasts—only skeletons of dead fae, like the one she'd taken her clothing from.

His lips parted and this time she placed a finger on Jack's mouth. To shush *him*. Even though she hadn't meant to do it, the movement was a habit. Jack's warm breath struck her digit and her nerves lit up everywhere, so she hurried and dropped her hand.

Ozma then explained Dorothy's story—how she was really a fae named Thelia, and how she'd defeated Langwidere. She continued to explain how Reva had been cursed as the Wicked Witch of the West and was traveling with Crow to defeat Locasta. Or at least she hoped Crow had caught up to her.

Jack's brow furrowed, confused. "News reached here from across the Sands, but I never really listened."

"Why not?" Ozma ducked under a branch and stopped when her foot pressed onto a blue bricked road, similar to the yellow one. A layer of dust coated the faded bricks, but not a single crack or fracture marred them.

"Because I never plan to go there anyway." Jack helped her lift the cart over the edge of the bricks and changed the subject. "What about your parents? Tip always wondered about them."

He was right. As Tip, she always had, but as Ozma she knew what had happened to them from Reva. King Pastoria and Queen Lurline. While thinking about them—regal images without faces—she didn't feel the way she thought she should, as a daughter, as a queen. If Ozma had known them, she would have loved them, but there was only the want to be sad, not the true, fragile emotion. "They're dead." She sighed. "The Wizard killed my father and Langwidere took the head of my mother to wear as her own."

Jack made a coughing sound. "I'm sorry, *what*?"

"I'll tell you all about Langwidere and her collection of heads later." Ozma had seen Crow burying them outside Glinda's castle. She'd wondered if her mother's had been in the collection or if Langwidere had already destroyed it.

His face turned serious. "I'm sorry you and Tip didn't get to know them."

She nodded, wishing she had.

As they rounded a curve up ahead, past fruit trees, light gray smoke curled upward. There were huts spread all across the land. Not in a single neat row, but anywhere and everywhere. The blue bricks led them closer and closer, and she found the huts to be neat and tidy. Emerald green leaves and dark purple branches made up the roofs, and each home was painted shades of yellow and red.

Her eyes widened at everything around her: the elves in front of their homes washing clothing in large silver buckets, the tiny fauns chasing each other in some sort of game, and another fae who looked to be preparing to go to the market with a cart full of flowered headdresses.

This part of Loland was much different than the stories she'd heard from Jack. He'd thought it drab, but perhaps that was because he'd seen it so many times and she hadn't. Even though he'd been compelled, he had still seen some of the world.

"You really were telling the truth about being hidden away," Jack said, his voice soft.

Had he truly not believed the story she'd just told him? She peered at him, his hazel irises shining, a glimpse of a smile forming on his lips, the first she'd seen from him since she'd been back.

Her annoyance vanished and she mirrored his smile. "I told you I was."

"Yes, you *told* me." Jack adjusted the crate as they passed a group of laughing fae. "But now I see it, Blossom. The way the world is dancing in your eyes."

She shrugged, not sure of what else to say.

A sweet scent hit her nose, and a large grassy area covered in wagons and carts caught her attention. Merchants chatting, customers purchasing what they needed.

As she passed the sellers, she observed each item they had. One fae stitched a cotton dress while another rolled a spool of spider silk. Sugary pastries, buttery rolls, meats, fruits, glass figurines, sapphire rings, ruby necklaces, tools, jeweled swords. So much, and too much—she wanted to run her fingertips across *everything*.

Jack grasped her by the shoulders and turned her in a different direction. "This way, Blossom. We want to make coin sometime today. Not tomorrow."

Ozma rolled her eyes and followed him down a lopsided path. "Why haven't you left the patch for good since the barrier is gone?"

"I'm saving up." He bit his lip. "Actually, it's not just that. I've practically been there my whole life. Tip and I always wanted to leave but now that I can… It sounds strange but I don't know, maybe it's the nostalgia. The pumpkins are all I know."

The past conversations between Tip and Jack came to her mind—the wishes, the dreams, and the death of those things. But she could relate to Jack on that level. It was all Jack had ever known, but he couldn't stay there forever. "Seeds, Jack. *Seeds*. Take them and run before Mombi returns and the barrier goes back up."

Before he could answer, a merchant called his name. "Jack! Hurry. I just sold the last pumpkin and had to send two customers away. My other items don't sell as fast." The centaur's arms were covered in beaded bracelets and golden loops decorated his ears. Dark green hair was braided down his back and his yellow gaze focused on Ozma, scanning her up and down. "Who's this?"

"His lover," Ozma rushed out. He wouldn't recognize her name, but that didn't mean it couldn't somehow get to the Wizard or Mombi before she had a chance to end them. She needed the element of surprise if she had any hope of succeeding.

Jack wrinkled his nose, looking at her strangely and then

must have decided to take pity on her because he answered nonchalantly, "This is Blossom. And no, you can't have her. I don't share." One of his long fingers trailed down her arm and she suppressed a shiver.

"A beautiful blossom indeed." The centaur grinned, then motioned to the baskets of oranges behind him, propped on a small table. "You want to buy any? Half price today."

"You mean every day. But no." Jack set his crate on the ground beside the centaur and unloaded the pumpkins into empty buckets in front of the wagon.

Ozma did the same with her cart as the centaur fished out a handful of coins and handed them to Jack.

He told the centaur he'd see him later, then pocketed the coins and placed the crate in the basket before pulling it along.

Ozma rushed up to him. "You didn't let me look around."

"That's because the bastard tries to get you to buy goods so he doesn't have to pay for the pumpkins. But we can look around if you want."

"No, perhaps another time." She needed to focus on getting back and doing the location spell anyway.

As they rounded a wagon with a brownie inside playing a flute and selling glass chimes, thunder boomed from the sky. Within moments, the rain started to pour, soaking them from head to toe.

"Told you it would rain," Ozma said, liking the feel of the light pellets against her skin. Even in the patch, she and Jack would work during storms. Mombi had made them, but Ozma never minded.

"Have you not seen that either?" He side-eyed her, running a finger across his well-formed lips.

"Of course I have!" The last time had been them naked together in the rain. And that had happened time and time again.

They stayed in comfortable silence, the only sound coming from the rain and tiny creatures scurrying for shelter, until they reached Jack's hut. The sky cleared as soon as they got to the entrance, as if by magic. He left the cart outside and pulled open the door for Ozma.

Beads of water slid down Jack's face and neck as he grabbed a bottle of homemade pumpkin ale from the table. He took a deep swig, not looking at Ozma. "Want some?" he asked.

She'd never drank alcohol before. Only pumpkin cider or water, but it was time for her to try new things. With a nod, she grabbed the bottle and took a long drink. A burning heat lit up her tongue and throat, causing her to cough. "Maybe not," she rasped, shoving the bottle back to him.

"Ah, not a fan, huh?" Jack smiled, and it dropped almost as quickly as it appeared. Clearing his throat, he stepped toward the door. "I'm going to gather more pumpkins to bring to the market later. You can come if you want."

This was the perfect opportunity she needed. "I think I'm going to lie down for a while. My wounds are aching a bit."

"Do you need me to change the bandages?" He reached out as if he meant to check for himself.

"No!" she practically shouted, then softer, "No."

"All right," he said with an amused smile. Then his lips slowly turned downward. "You're going to rest, right? If I leave you alone? You won't go back to the lake or do anything else to cause trouble? I won't be here to save you …"

"I'll rest," she lied.

With a nod, Jack went out the front door, and Ozma waited several moments before heading to the back of the room. After packing up her satchel with fruit, she slowly drew up the bedroom window and hurried to slip outside. Checking each direction, she darted into the forest behind the hut so she would be hidden by trees. She took out her dagger as she rushed to Mombi's, remaining vigilant in case a dangerous creature appeared like the night before.

Ozma avoided any crackling leaves until she'd made it safely to the area behind Mombi's hut. She peered around a tilted tree with decaying limbs, and spotted Jack, his back turned, seeming to be gutting a pumpkin.

Before Jack had time to turn around, she lunged out of the trees toward the front of the hut and pulled open the door, not making a single sound as she pressed inside.

The scent of Mombi's past concoctions hit her nose again as she entered the witch's bedroom. She took the pages she'd torn out of the book from her satchel. First, Ozma gathered a bucket and filled it with pumpkin water. Mombi kept at least ten jugs of the stuff in the sitting room at a time. The cabinet was only half full of the jars it usually held, most likely due to Mombi taking some with her on the journey. She then gathered a few strands of Mombi's hair—the something personal—still stuck to her pillow, followed by gremlin blood and salamander feet.

Finally, she lifted her dagger and pressed it to the flesh of her ankle. She bit the inside of her cheek when she pushed in and sliced off a sliver of flesh. A low squeal escaped her lips as she tossed the skin into the bucket. The last things she needed were her saliva and blood, so she spat into the pail and used a few drops of scarlet from her throbbing ankle before bandaging it with cloth from a pile of clothing.

As she stirred the liquid with a wooden spoon, she chanted the words from the spell book page. A blue light flickered, and she chewed her lip as she poured a small amount of the mixture into a vial. Gripping the glass, she chanted the words again.

The blue light became a thin line, like yarn unraveling, before shooting out of the area, and through the sitting room to outside, connecting her to Mombi. Ozma opened the front door and peeked out, finding the light stretching right past Jack as he loaded pumpkins into the cart. He wouldn't be able to see it—only she could.

Ozma couldn't wait until nightfall to go hunt down Mombi—she was going now. She hoped Jack wouldn't notice her as she dashed back into the forest and out of his view. Quickening her pace, she retraced her steps into the forest and flew through the trees, wondering how long it would take for her to get to Mombi.

Ozma said a goodbye to Jack inside her head, but it wasn't forever. She would see him again, at least to let him know she'd killed Mombi so he would be completely free. But her heart still felt heavy.

The light guided her past faeries circling overhead and other tree fae watching her from branches or inside trunks. Ozma didn't stop once, not until she reached the market. Fae kept asking her to purchase their goods, but she ignored them, until a female troll with deep wrinkles, and one eye lower than the other, grabbed her shoulders.

"Sit," she demanded and shoved Ozma down onto a velvet-padded chair.

"I don't have coin," Ozma said, trying to escape the hands clamping her into place. "I'm—I'm in a hurry."

"On me. Your hair is in much need of attention. It can easily be grabbed or unwillingly chopped off and sold."

Before Ozma could utter a word, the troll quickly braided her hair. She relaxed under the female's practiced movements as she effortlessly pressed braids into a crown around her head. The troll then plucked flowers from a painted vase and entwined them in sections of Ozma's hair.

"There." The troll clucked her tongue. "Much better."

Sliding her fingers into her satchel, Ozma drew out a fruit and handed it to the troll as payment anyway—the female had been right. Mombi didn't need any more advantages than she already had.

Ozma brushed a velvety petal in her hair and resumed following the light out of the market, down a long sloping hill. In the distance, more forestry and huts took up the area, but the light wasn't taking her there, it was leading her to the right, toward an unlit tunnel, reminding her of the dark place. Her heart hammered in her chest as she studied it for longer than she should have.

As she took a step forward, a strong hand hauled her back

against a solid chest. "I've let this charade go on long enough. What are you up to, Blossom?"

Chapter Eight

Jack

Jack dropped the handles of the cart in front of Antair's stall and stretched, his back popping three times. "That's it for the day," he told the centaur. And probably forever. There were smaller pumpkins left and, though he would've liked more coin first, Ozma was right. It was risky to stay too long and have Mombi return. Waiting another week was asking for trouble. He should run with as many seeds as he could. If he allowed himself to become her slave again—

No. He would never. There were other ways to fill his pockets, even if he had to whore professionally. He did enjoy a good fuck anyway, especially when it took his mind off things. It would still be better than being trapped in that damn field.

"I wish Mombi had left you some pies to bring before heading off," Antair lamented.

Jack shrugged. He wouldn't wish those pies on anyone. There was no telling what that fucking masochistic witch put in them. There were probably crystallized bat wings or petrified gnome shit mixed into the batter. He ate Mombi's cooking only when he *had* to, but here these fae were *missing her pies.* Probably due to some sort of addictive powder, as her skills over a fire were mediocre at best.

"Your friend from earlier isn't helping you this time?"

Jack shook his head. "She's at the farm." Sleeping, like he wished he was, though he regretted not checking on her before he left. Her wounds from the night before were deep and, though he'd put ointment on them for her, they still had to bother her a bit. He hadn't wanted to wake her by stepping on a creaking floorboard. Before going back, he should find a stall selling a potion to prevent infection and maybe some herbs for pain.

"Is she now?" the centaur asked with a mischievous grin.

"Yes." Jack narrowed his eyes. Why did it feel like Antair was implying something else? Ozma had lied and said they were lovers, so it couldn't be Antair hinting that there was *more* between them. When Antair only continued to smirk, Jack's patience snapped. "What aren't you telling me?"

"Oh nothing." His beaded bracelets clicked together as he lifted a pumpkin from the cart. "Only that she's sitting at Asie's right now, getting her hair braided."

Jack's heart nearly stopped. "She's … *what?*" he nearly shouted. But that might alert Ozma to his presence and he wanted to see what she was up to. How did she get past him? *When?* Why? If she wanted to get her hair done, there was no reason she couldn't simply *tell* him that she was going for a bit of pampering. After years of being trapped, he couldn't blame her, but why wouldn't she *tell him*?

Wait.

How was she paying for this? Jack patted his pockets and the heavy clink of coin from earlier sounded. He sighed, relieved, though it was stupid of him to work in the field with a pocket full of money, but the thought of leaving it unattended somewhere made him uneasy.

Antair chuckled and waved him off. "I'll watch your cart if you want to catch up with her."

Jack hesitated. He wanted to confront Ozma, but what right did he have? If she went to the market to have her hair braided, who was he to complain? She wasn't his prisoner. *She* is *a liar though.* And he'd just begun to believe her.

That's what you get, Jack.

Believe someone and they use it to ruin you.

"Thanks," Jack told Antair through a grimace. "I'll take you up on that, actually."

He wandered as casually as he could toward another part of the market. Food shops gave way to tables covered in rouge made from berries, then gems fashioned into jewelry. Clothing took up nearly half of the street: woven skirts, hooded jackets, hats, and boots. Then came artists inking skin, either permanently or with a paste that faded over a few weeks. Ozma sat at a booth nestled between a table covered in hat pins and a pixie who would pierce any part of a fae's body. Her back was to Jack as an elderly troll carefully arranged her golden locks. Tiny blue flowers that matched Ozma's dress were woven into the intricate braids.

Sneaky, Blossom.

She hadn't been joking when she'd said she had learned how to get around unnoticed.

Ozma stood, the troll having finished her work, and hefted a satchel from the ground. She quickly handed a piece of fruit to the troll before continuing down the bricked path. There looked to be a fresh pep in her step as she walked. Jack trailed her at a distance, his cart safe with Antair, to see what she was up to, but a troubled feeling came over him the farther they got from town. When Ozma paused to stare at a daunting black tunnel, the feeling only intensified.

Don't you dare, Blossom. I'm not ready to die yet.

And die they both would—probably. Jack would give them a five percent chance of survival if they went into that tunnel. Places like that were where fae went to conduct nefarious business such as trading younglings for coin or hiring an assassin.

Or to eat other fae who were conducting nefarious business.

They would be an easy snack for any number of bloodthirsty creatures. So what the hell was she doing? What reason could she possibly have to visit a place like this?

Ozma seemed to steel herself and took a step toward the tunnel.

Oh, fuck no!

Jack lunged forward and grabbed her wrist, hauling her back into his chest. "I've let this charade go on long enough. What are you up to, Blossom?"

She struggled against his hold, but Jack didn't give an inch, so she finally stilled. "What are you doing here, Jack?"

"Well, I *was* dropping more pumpkins off at the market, when what did I see?" He paused, though he didn't expect an answer. "You. Getting your hair braided when you claimed that your wounds were aching too much to help me."

"The rain ruined my hair," she said with forced casualness.

Jack spun her to face him, keeping a grip on her upper arms. "So, you walked all the way to town to get it fixed without a coin to your name? Don't fuck with me. What's going on?"

She studied his face, her blue eyes roaming over his features. He hoped she could tell how angry he was, hoped that his face showed the depth of the rage. She lied again and again. Put herself in danger. But mostly, he was upset that he wanted so badly to trust her. That she got under his skin so much. And Tip… Jack would never forgive himself if anything happened to his sister.

When her gaze met his again, she appeared completely emotionless.

What am I doing? *Why do I care?*

Why is she doing this to me? Stirring up old feelings. Playing games with him. It wasn't fair, nor was it in the least bit kind. He'd had enough cruelty in his life to allow for any more.

Jack growled. "Speak."

"I don't know what you want to hear," she said quietly.

"The truth!" he demanded. "You storm onto the farm, lie to my face, then get it in your head to run off—through *that* tunnel, no less—and you think I don't deserve to know what you're doing here? What if I hadn't found you and you'd died? What then? I would be forced to wonder what happened to Tip's sister for the rest of my life. Forced to worry if you were still out there, in pain, and if there was something I could do to stop it."

"Okay, okay," Ozma said quickly. "I'm going to kill Mombi. Happy now?"

Happy? Was he fucking *happy* that she was embarking on a journey to get herself killed? "You are nothing like your brother," he seethed.

Ozma's jaw dropped. "Wh... What's that supposed to mean?"

"He was never this insufferable," Jack snapped, letting go of her arms. "Or this stupid."

"Perhaps because he was *trapped* in that patch. Perhaps you didn't truly know him," she retorted.

How dare she... Clenching his jaw, he stormed around her toward the tunnel and kept going without looking back. He was nearly halfway to the entrance when Ozma caught up.

"What are you doing?" she asked.

"Going with you. Obviously."

"You can't—"

"I can do whatever the fuck I want, Blossom. No one has a claim over me anymore." Not since Mombi's barrier dropped and Tip died. Jack was a completely free fae—his body *and* his heart.

He picked up the pace, making it to the foreboding tunnel much faster than he expected. It was eerily silent there. Long, sweeping vines swooped down over the oblong entrance and moss clung to the large rocks peeking out from the packed dirt. A musty, metallic scent wafted from inside.

"You don't have to come," Ozma whispered.

Jack ground his teeth together and reached down to grab a

thick branch from the dirt. It was better than going in there with only a small carving knife, dull from use on so many pumpkins. At least the branch gave him range. "I wish that were true, but Tip would never forgive me. And that I *do know* about him."

Ozma looked up at him, blinking, unspoken words filling the space between them. Jack cleared his throat to distract himself from studying the shape of her lips. He was having *none* of that bullshit. Did he want answers? Yes. Did he have an unexplainable urge to kiss some sense into her? Also, yes. But, that was a hard no. If only she were anyone besides Tip's sister...

"Damn," he muttered and headed inside the tunnel. He had to calm himself before he did or said something completely moronic.

Before the light faded behind them, he took note of the thick wooden beams running across the ceiling and down both sides of the tunnel, holding everything up safely. *The only safe thing in here,* he thought. Scratching sounds filled the darkness. Dubious laughter bubbled. A muffled scream.

There was no telling if the creatures lurking around them could see in the dark or not. But on the off chance the predators were equally blind as them, there was no sense giving away their position with a light.

"This way," Ozma whispered, tugging him along, when they'd been walking for what felt like hours.

Jack stumbled over something on the ground—a root perhaps, or a severed body part. He winced at the thought. "How do you know? I can't see shit."

"I used a spell before I left the patch," she admitted.

Jack stumbled to a halt. "A spell? One of *Mombi's* spells? Is *that* what you were looking for in her room the other night?"

There was a long pause before Ozma asked, "You followed me? That's how you saved me at the lake."

"Of course, I followed you. Not only do I not trust you, but you went out the window. There's no reason to sneak about unless you're up to no good." He huffed out a breath. "But to use one of Mombi's spells? She uses dark magic—tinkers with forces that should never be messed with."

"It's just a tracking spell," she scoffed. "It's leading me to Mombi with a trail of light."

A tracking spell using *dark magic.* That was probably why nothing dared attack them—the beasts could sense whatever evil was at work. But it was too late to talk Ozma out of it, so he kept his thoughts to himself. "This isn't some wild guess, then?"

Ozma snorted softly. "Not so stupid after all, am I?"

"Don't go getting ahead of yourself, Blossom. This is still foolish."

"Say that again when she's dead." Ozma gripped Jack's hand and steered him in the right direction as the tunnel curved.

"Let's make a deal." Jack squeezed her hand, feeling a little more comfortable touching her when he couldn't see a fucking thing. Her skin was smooth, though callouses dotted the pads of her palm. They were smaller than his but no less prevalent. "If she dies and we don't, I'll take back what I said."

"Which part?"

Was … that hurt in her voice? He had been angry with her and lashed out, but he hadn't meant what he said. Not really. His mind was being pulled in a million directions. Believe her, or don't? Trust her, or don't? Help her or… *No.* That one he was certain of. He was helping her whether she wanted him to or not. But he wished that it didn't feel as if she were keeping something important from him. Wished she would lay everything out—her motive, how she knew her way around the farm so well…

"All of it, Blossom," he answered.

"Good. Because she's there."

Jack jerked, expecting the witch to be standing directly in front of them, but instead noticed a faint trickle of sunlight. They were almost at the other end of the tunnel now—completely unscathed, physically. Having unseen fae hissing and growling at him from the darkness had his hand shaking around the branch. The knife in his boot would only be helpful if something was close enough for him to use it, though he didn't want to wield either weapon if he could help it.

Nothing attacked. Just threatened to. It felt impossible. There were creatures in there and the two of them were practically defenseless. Something didn't feel right, but nothing involving dark magic ever did.

Still, he followed Ozma through the last bit of tunnel and out into the light once more. Though, *light* was a stretch. The sun was half obscured by land with night hot on its heels, and the realization that they would be stuck out there hit Jack for the first time. He'd never spent an entire evening away from the farm before.

Ozma gave a hard yank on Jack's hand and they tumbled into the prickly brush.

"Shit," he mumbled as a particularly pointy thorn scratched his arm. Blood welled on his skin. "Why did you do that?"

"There," Ozma whispered, pointing overhead at a large overhang made from rock. "We have to climb."

As if going through the tunnel wasn't bad enough, now they had to climb over it? *Fuck...* He held back a groan as he stood, hands on his hips, watching Ozma hike effortlessly up the steep hillside. It was only when she disappeared onto the overhang that he scrambled up after her, dropping his branch. When he reached her side, hunched behind a fallen log, they both peered wordlessly over the bark as the soft padding of hooves struck the ground.

A familiar blue and maroon wagon, the wood curved in an arc over the bed of it, came around a bend with a gray stag pulling it. And, holding onto the reins, was Mombi, wearing the same clothes she'd left in. Jack swallowed hard at the sight of her. What were they thinking, confronting her? Both he and Ozma ducked down when the wagon neared. As it passed their hiding place, Jack caught a whiff of the smokey scent of burning wood mixed with the acrid odor of burning hair.

Up to your dark magic, as always, you horrid bitch.

The wagon creaked to a stop and Jack held his breath, peeking out again, sure she'd seen them. But Mombi didn't seem at all fazed. She hummed off-tune as she leapt down from the seat with all the grace of a newborn foal, nearly falling. The witch caught herself on the spokes of the mud-slicked wheel and shifted a small woven basket over her arm. With her other hand, she removed her cloak and placed it on the bench where she had been sitting.

Each of her steps came with a grunt as if it pained her to move. It probably did. She'd left the farm to help the Wizard, which meant she was using her magic more often. Probably daily. By seeing her again, it hit Jack just how much of a fool he'd been to stay at the farm. Money could be made anywhere—not just from pumpkins.

Setting her basket down on the steps leading into the rear of the wagon, she pulled a large cleaver from her skirts. "Yes, yes," she mumbled to herself, trailing her thumb over the blade. "Sharp enough. Now…"

The witch turned her gaze to the top of the wagon. Jack's eyes traveled upward to see what was so interesting and froze. Sprites in cages. Dozens of them hung along the sides of the wagon like decorations. As if sensing Jack's stare, the sprites started screaming, their weak voices somehow still sounding like a crack of thunder across the small clearing.

"Help! Please, sir, help us!"

A chorus of cries, all directed at him.

"Fuck," he breathed.

Mombi looked over her shoulder and her beady stare landed directly on him where he still watched over the fallen tree. "Jack!" she screeched so loud it hurt his ears. "How did you get off the farm?"

She hadn't realized the barrier fell?

Fuck, fuck, fuck, fuck, fu—

"Get over here, you disobedient little bastard!"

As Jack stood, resigned to the witch's wrath, a rock flew

through the air and pelted Mombi right in the temple. She flailed about for a moment before using her powers to balance herself. Regaining her composure, she blasted her magic in the direction the rock had come from.

And hit the empty ground.

"Time to go," he said quickly while Mombi was distracted by some miracle attack. He glanced down to hurry Ozma back the way they'd come … only to find himself alone.

"No." His eyes shot up, scouring the area. Mombi appeared to be the only fae there. *Where are you, Blossom?*

Another rock.

Another answering blast of power.

He caught a flash of blue fabric dart behind a wide tree.

Stupid female—I'm never taking back what I said! Never! Foolish, impulsive—

Mombi's power wrapped around Jack's throat and dragged him forward. He clawed at the invisible hand, choking, his heart thumping wildly. "Jack, Jack, Jack," she scolded. "You should've run when you had the chance."

He should have. Should have run and never looked back.

And now he was as good as dead.

"Come out here or I'll kill him!" Mombi screamed.

There was a long moment where nothing happened. Nothing but the fading of color. From the sunset? *If only.* Stars sparked in his vision. Air. He needed air. But he hoped Ozma wouldn't rise to the bait. If she ran, saved herself, then he would gladly die. He had nothing to live for anyway, so if he could save Tip's sister on the way out…

"I'm here," Ozma called. When she stepped out from her hiding place, appearing as a blue blur with golden hair, Jack's heart dropped.

"Ozma?" Mombi hissed in surprise, her eyes impossibly wide. "You're not supposed to be here…"

"Let him go," she commanded.

"I think I'll kill him instead." Mombi's grip tightened. "Then

I'll shrink you to the size of a doll and keep you locked in a box."

Jack's hands went numb, his arms too heavy to keep clawing pointlessly at his neck. The world was fading. Fading, fading…

Mombi let out a loud squeal at the same time a deafening *boom* sounded. Her magic released him and he fell to the grass, gasping desperately for air. With a quick glance, he saw the wide tree tilt. It fell in slow motion, one branch tumbling, dragging down another and another.

"Got you," Mombi crowed.

Jack's gaze instantly cleared at the words as the adrenaline kicked in. Mombi had Ozma by the throat, holding her three feet off the ground, while her other hand moved in a swirling motion. *A spell.*

Jack watched the air darken around Mombi's fingers. His chest became so tight he was sure it would crack open against the roaring beat of his heart. Knees shaking, he climbed to his feet and threw a hand out. "Stop!"

A swirl of green, blue, and yellow burst from his palm. *What the fuck is this?* But there was really only one logical answer: *magic.* The pressure of it nearly snapped the bones in his hand, but he was too shocked to do anything other than stare.

He watched as vines curled forward from the trees and snapped around Mombi's limbs. As grass grew higher and higher around her body. The witch screamed as a tree branch extended downward, piercing her through the shoulder. Blood immediately seeped into the fabric around the wound.

Ozma dropped to the ground in his peripheral, but he couldn't drag his attention away from the scene before him. The witch shrieked again as the grass cocooned her. The vines went taut, pulling her arms and legs. Her cries became muffled as the grass tightened.

Jack's breaths came in heavy pants and his weak legs buckled. He tried to pull his hand back, close it into a fist before whatever was happening killed him too. But it revolted. Forced more, more, *more*, from him.

Until the vines ripped each of Mombi's limbs from her body. Blood shot out like geysers, coating the grass around her. Jack's mind went blank at the sight. Crimson dotted the area. Pooled around the body. The grass-wrapped witch tumbled back in slow motion, rolling slightly when she finally hit the ground, and the magic retreated into his palm.

Dead. Mombi was dead.

Jack shouted in triumph. He'd killed her! *Fucking yes, I did!* But the excitement was short lived as his body quivered with exhaustion. A hollowness spread through him. Used up.

"Jack!" Ozma shouted.

At least, he thought she did. His hearing had followed his vision—fading and fading and fading…

Chapter Nine

Ozma

Mombi was dead. But so was Jack. Ozma let out a choked sob and rushed to Jack's side. Beads of perspiration lined his brows, his hair damp and skin pale. Even his freckles seemed faded.

All around her, plants had sprung up, grown in size, like nothing she'd ever seen before, not even at the pumpkin patch where only the crop grew unnaturally fast. Whatever it was had come from Jack, his outstretched hand. *Magic.* But how?

Ozma couldn't think straight as she shook his shoulders. "Damn it, Jack, come on! Wake up, so you can say you don't trust me again. Wake up, so I can tell you how much I love you!"

Jack's eyes remained closed as she pressed her palm to his chest. *Thump thump. Thump thump.* His heart beat rhythmically against her hand, his chest gently rising. A soft groan escaped his lips, but his lids stayed shut. Had he broken out of a curse, the way she had? She'd always assumed Jack didn't have magic, but in the dark place she'd wondered if Mombi had done something nefarious to him too. And she'd been right.

Screams exploded from the wagon behind her. She whirled around to the dozens and dozens of sprites locked in iron cages.

Their bright wings were unable to flap with the tight fit of how many Mombi had shoved inside together.

The enclosed wagon was light blue, and a curving arch accentuated it, while the front was painted maroon, with gold flowers and emerald vines crawling up its length. A gray stag stood harnessed to the wagon, appearing ready to lead it if commanded.

"Mombi carries the key on her," a female sprite, with light pink hair, chirped, pointing in the direction of the witch. "In her left pocket."

Ozma peered up at the darkening sky—night would be falling soon. Too soon. The blue light tracking Mombi had vanished once Jack ended the witch's life. She'd secretly hoped that the Wizard would've been there too. It would be impossible to perform another location spell because she had nothing of his. But one dead was better than none.

Pulling the dagger from her waist, Ozma held it up as she padded toward Mombi. She would free the trapped sprites, then get Jack loaded in the wagon so she could bring him home before figuring out a plan to find the Wizard. It was lucky that Mombi had been so close, but they couldn't risk staying on the farm for much longer. Not when the Wizard could come looking for the dead witch.

The grass still cocooned Mombi's body—or what was left of it. All her limbs had been ripped away, the ground soaked in scarlet. Ozma lifted her blade and swiped a clean line down from the top of the witch's head to her navel. Mombi's bloodshot eyes stared blankly up at the sky. She hadn't gotten to kill her, but she pierced her weapon through Mombi's heart anyway and released a scream of her own. "You *bitch*!" One melancholic cry that spoke of despair over missed opportunities, a life that could have been more for her, for Jack. Then she slammed her hand across the dead witch's cheek like Mombi had done to her so many times.

Tears slid down Ozma's cheeks and she brushed them away.

She wiped the blood from her dagger on Mombi's tattered dress, then placed it back at her waist. A raised outline of an object in the left pocket, over Mombi's breast, caught her eye. Ozma fished out the silver key.

She walked back to the wagon, stopping at the first iron cage. "Tell me," Ozma asked the pink-haired sprite, "do you know which direction Mombi came from, and where the Wizard is staying?"

"She journeyed from the seaport after going to Orkland. That's where he is." The sprite paused and shook her head. "But you don't want to go to Orkland. Everyone there is under an enchantment, doing what the Wizard orders."

Ozma remembered the maps Jack drew of the places outside Loland. Orkland was an island, not too far from here. Just go through Hiland and sail across. She could feel the correct path in her veins but not where the port was along the sea.

"I have to go." Ozma shrugged. Of course Oz wouldn't be in Loland anymore. "Which way leads to the seaport?" With a sigh, careful to avoid touching the iron, she unlocked each cage, one by one.

The sprite hesitated but rattled off the directions.

Loosening her shoulders, Ozma peered at Jack and hoped she could lift him into the wagon. Once they arrived back at the farm, she would have to gather more supplies and spells before heading to Orkland. She didn't know if she would leave him there or if he would decide to come with her once he was awake. He had come with her to stop Mombi… She wasn't going to sneak off again, and he'd earned the right to choose whether he wanted to accompany her or not. The truth was, she wouldn't mind spending more time with him.

Ozma went to the wagon door and opened it. Something burst out, shoving her aside, and she let out a scream. A hobgoblin flopped to the ground as she caught herself. He rolled with a growl, dried blood caked around a half-missing ear. He got up to run, and tripped, his hands bound behind his back.

"Wait," Ozma said. "I'll untie you."

The hobgoblin stopped and slowly turned around, eyeing her with suspicion. "She took my ear. Wanted my arms next."

Ozma calmly nodded. "Not anymore. She's dead." Taking out her dagger, she walked toward him and cut the rope. "There, you're free."

"What do I owe you? Though I suppose, now that I'm unbound, it's enough that I don't eat you." He cocked his head, staring at her like he wanted to rip out her heart and feast on it.

A shiver ran down her spine at the thought of his filthy hand thrusting inside her chest. She shook off the image, pulled back her shoulders, and motioned at Jack. "Help me put him in the wagon and I'll consider it a fair trade."

With a low grunt, the hobgoblin stumbled toward Jack and lifted his legs while Ozma hauled him under his arms. She was close to Jack's height, but he still wasn't light enough for her to carry.

Inside the wagon, mold permeated the air. Amidst dried herbs, was mostly empty space, aside from a stack of books in the corner and two baskets full of fruit, some rotten.

After they placed Jack on the floor, Ozma shut the door and the hobgoblin grunted again as he scurried off into the woods—most likely to find something to shred apart.

At the front of the wagon was a teal wooden plank to sit on with Mombi's cloak sprawled out along the edge. Something hard poked at Ozma when she sank onto the cloak. Crinkling her nose, she tugged out a shiny red stone in the shape of a heart. "Strange." If Mombi'd had it in her cloak, perhaps it could be useful. She shoved the stone into her satchel and tossed the cloak on the ground.

Grabbing the reins to the stag, she snapped them for the beast to go. The stag didn't move.

"Oh, come on!" she screamed, the crescent moon already pushing up into the night sky. Nothing. The stubborn beast just sat there with its chin lifted.

From her satchel, Ozma took out a purple fruit, then hopped down to go to the stag. He leaned forward, his antlers almost brushing her face as he sniffed at the fruit, finally biting into it. Ozma quickly pulled her hand back, not allowing him another taste. "I'll give you the rest once we get home." A huff of air escaped his nostrils as she hopped back onto the plank, bringing down the reins once more.

This time the stag stomped his feet and dragged the wagon forward with a jolt. Ozma's back struck the wagon, and she straightened in her seat. As they moved through the dark, the wagon bobbed side to side, and she hoped Jack would be all right in there until they got home.

Ozma wished the vial's light still worked, the way it had when they went through the tunnel earlier. What Jack hadn't known was that the blue light from the magical line had lit up the area for her. She'd seen what was in there. The beasts clinging to the walls, blood staining their mouths and sharp teeth, hissing, prepared to strike. But they hadn't. She thought it had something to do with the light from the vial, like they were afraid of it, even though she wasn't sure if they could see it.

The stag pulled the wagon into the tunnel and Ozma shivered, the inky black sweeping closed like a curtain around her. It wouldn't take too dreadfully long for them to get out, but what if one of the creatures decided to attack? As if in answer to her thoughts, hissing reverberated off the walls. A hard thump dropped down on top of the wagon, rattling it, and Ozma yanked out her dagger. But she couldn't see a damn thing.

A small body landed beside her, the plank she sat on shaking as sharp talons clawed her arm. She thrust her blade into whatever part of the creature it was, and the beast released an agonized howl. Another crashed behind her onto the wagon. As she prepared her dagger again, a bright light swirled around her, and for a moment, she thought it was from her, that her magic had returned.

But it hadn't.

Before her, the gray stag glowed a bright yellow, body and antlers, lighting up the tunnel like rays of sunshine. The creatures hissed, baring their fangs, rumpling their wings as they scurried up the walls. Their spines protruded through their thin skin, and she wasn't sure if they even had any eyes. The light yellow of the stag turned to a pale blue, shining, and he continued straight down the path, unbothered. All the while, the creatures growled, driving their talons at the walls in rage.

"You saved us," Ozma said in awe as she watched the colors of the stag change from one shade to another. His brightness remained until they exited the tunnel, then the hue dimmed to his usual light gray.

As they traveled toward the market, it was mostly quiet. A couple of fae with curling horns outside a wagon were groping each other while kissing. Shops stood dark and empty. Lit lanterns hung on several of the wagons where the owners were probably sleeping inside, waiting to begin again the following day.

The sliver of moon shone brighter than before, the sky full of twinkling stars as they rode off the bricked road and entered the forest toward the patch. Ozma thought again about Jack. It had to be the same thing that had happened to her. Perhaps he'd been angry enough to break free from whatever curse Mombi had placed upon him.

She wondered, if Jack hadn't been there, would she have been able to kill Mombi on her own? That was the second time he'd saved her since she'd been back in Oz. It seemed she was always being rescued. Even Reva had defeated all the Wheelers, aside from the one that was an easy kill for Ozma. She'd escaped the dark place because of Thelia. With the beasts in the Sands, she'd only gotten away because one had attacked the other. A tinge of doubt spread through her that maybe she couldn't defeat the Wizard. Not without Jack or Reva or Thelia. Or a color-changing stag, apparently…

Blowing out an exaggerated breath, Ozma pulled on the reins

as they neared Jack's hut. When the wagon came to a stop, she leapt to the grass and released the stag from his binds.

"Go wherever you wish." Ozma took out the fruit from earlier and gave it to him, then moved toward the wagon door. A nudge came at her arm, the stag following her. "Are you still hungry? I'll give you more fruit if you help us on one more journey."

The stag stomped its feet against the ground and threw back its head as if in agreement.

"There's a creek we passed, if you want to get something to drink. We'll leave in the morning, but only if Jack is all right." The stag seemed to understand, but studied her for a long moment before venturing toward the forest.

Ozma clasped the handle to the wagon door and drew it open, finding Jack still asleep on his back. What if it wasn't fatigue from using his magic that made him sleep? What if Mombi had cast a dark spell with her last breath and he never woke up?

Stepping inside the wagon, she knelt next to him. Jack groaned, his shoulders moving, like he was trying to stir himself from a nightmare. Out the door, a sizzling sounded, growing louder and closer by the second. She surveyed the patch, and her eyes widened. Around the wagon, the vegetation started to grow, spread. Shadows shifted as pumpkins bloomed to full-size, some getting bigger and bigger, larger than she'd ever seen.

She shook Jack wildly, attempting to wake him before things got completely out of hand. "Jack!" she shouted.

He jerked forward, his eyes bursting open, settling on her. Clasping her wrist, his voice came out raspy. "It was a dream..."

Ozma glanced out the door, at the hovering silhouettes from the giant pumpkins. "No, Jack. It wasn't."

Chapter Ten

Jack

The night passed in a haze of fever sweats and vivid dreams. In one, Jack had a pumpkin for a head and a chicken for a friend. Another forced him to watch Tip explode into dust over and over again. All were fucking terrible, but Ozma never left his side. She was there with a cool cloth for his forehead or to run her fingers through his damp hair to calm him.

Jack watched her now. She had pulled one of his rickety dining chairs to his bedside and rested her head on the mattress beside his thighs. There was a vague memory of waking inside a wagon and her insisting the events that had played out weren't a dream. Then he'd stumbled inside with her help and collapsed again on the bed.

It was a shock to find out that Mombi had suppressed his powers. That he *had* powers. That was the only reason he could think of for what had happened—fae didn't often gain abilities after maturity. He had always thought he was born without magic, but to have it blast out of him like that… And for that magic to deliver such a bloody death. Even now his muscles ached. His head was clear though. Clear enough to know that

Mombi was finally fucking dead.

Breaking out of a curse is a bitch, though.

Jack had left his cart at the market, but he didn't give a shit about that now. He eased himself up with a soft grunt, and flicked the tip of Ozma's pointed ear. She leapt up with a squeak. *Cute.* Jack grinned and his chapped lips cracked slightly.

"Jack?" She rubbed the sleep from her eyes. "How are you feeling?"

"Better," he said. He felt less heavy and his breaths didn't hurt like they had the night before.

She let out a relieved sigh. "You had me worried."

"Sorry, Blossom. You won't be rid of me that easily."

Ozma rolled her eyes and stood, stretching her back. Jack didn't bother to hide that his gaze was drawn to her chest with the movement. What could he say? He was a horny bastard. No matter how many fae he was with, no one truly satisfied his hunger since Tip. She crossed her arms and glared down at him, spearing him with a trace amount of guilt. *Tip's sister*, he reminded himself again.

"I'd apologize but…" He shrugged.

"I'd smack you if you hadn't just been at death's door."

"Don't exaggerate," he said.

Ozma swatted lightly at him. "Are you hungry?"

"Famished, but I need a bath more than food." He could smell himself—old sweat and dirt—so he knew it was bad, and he hated feeling sticky. "Pack a lunch and meet me at the lake. We'll have ourselves a celebratory picnic."

Ozma lifted the chair, assumedly to return it to the table, and shot him a glare. "The lake with the undine?"

Jack lifted his lips in a knowing smirk. "Exactly."

"Ah, okay. I see. You have a death wish." She set the chair back down.

"Don't worry, Blossom." Jack flung the thin blanket off and stood slowly, testing his strength. *Back to normal.* "I won't get in the water until she's dead."

"And I suppose you're up to fishing her out of there?"

"I've never been good at catching fish." He was going to test his magic. It flowed through him now like a second set of veins, and he was curious to see what he could do with it. Make sure he was able to summon and control it. If there were ever a time when he needed to use it, like with Mombi, he wanted to be sure he could. "Go on. The fare is up to you."

"Are you sure this is a good idea?"

Jack bopped her on the nose as he passed wordlessly out of the bedroom. Was he sure? Hell no. But he was going to have fun testing his limits.

Outside, over-sized pumpkins dotted the field as a testament to his strength. Physical proof that everything had actually happened the night before. Excitement fluttered through his stomach.

The path to the lake felt extra long with the sun high, air crisp, and leaves just beginning to change color. Not because of his slight aches and pains, but because he wanted to unleash himself. His fingers flexed at his sides as he tried to conjure up a spark of magic on the way. The power beneath his skin stirred, but it seemed trapped.

When Jack reached the lake, he stopped a few feet from the still water. "Okay," he told himself. Maybe he simply had to hold out his hand again. He scanned the grass until he found a small yellow flower with liquid droplets resting on its petals. Pointing his palm at the flower, he pushed at the magic. Nothing happened.

Seemed too easy anyway.

Grow, he thought at the flower, trying to be more specific. Still nothing.

Again and again he *tried.*

Again and again he *failed.* It had come so naturally before…

Releasing a sigh, Jack plopped to the ground. "Please grow," he whispered, coaxing the little bud to bloom bigger. A tiny bit of the pressure left his palm, easing the tension that built there, and the flower shot up an inch.

"A-ha!" he cried and jumped to his feet. "That's more like it!"

"Amazing," Ozma said in awe from behind him, and he whirled around. When had she shown up? "Do it again."

Jack took a deep breath and, using his magic, coaxed the flower to rise even higher. Again it worked. Biting his lip, he closed his eyes and spread his magic wider. He held up his hands, the magic begging the grass to grow, and every blade woke as his power touched them. It was like a thousand butterfly wings brushing through him. Fluttering faster and faster until he felt numb to all other sensations.

Ozma inhaled, an impressed sound, and grabbed his elbow.

Jack snapped his eyes open to find the grass along the lake was nearly as tall as they were. *Oh shit.* "I guess I got a little carried away," he said. But that was fine. It would take practice to perfect.

"Maybe a little," Ozma drawled with a light laugh.

"There's one more thing I want to try," he told her in a serious voice.

"What?"

"Killing the undine." Because it was *his* lake, so where better to try?

Ozma said nothing as he turned toward the water and focused his power on the plant life swaying at the bottom of the lake. He didn't ask any of it to grow—not until he found a patch of grass near the center that felt trampled upon. *The undine's nest.* While he couldn't see it, he knew the undine was lying there. Sleeping or, perhaps, just waiting patiently for prey to enter the water, but the weight of her body was suffocating the plant life.

Now, he would turn the tables.

Grow, he thought at the swaying grass along the edge of the nest. *Grow and hold her.*

The grass lengthened, knitting together into a net around the undine. He felt the creature as if the grass was his own skin.

Tighten. As tight as you can. Cover her gills. Immobilize her hands.

And the grass did. Phantom movements echoed against his palm. Air bubbles rose to the surface in what Jack imagined were the undine's dying screams. The last bits of air squeezed from her lungs, her gills unable to bring in any more. He held the power in place until the strain of the undine's struggles ceased. Then he held it some more just to be safe.

"There," he said after a handful of moments, and released the magic. "She's dead."

His body shook slightly, the aches worse than before, but he hadn't blacked out. *A damn improvement.* He knew that so much more would be possible once he learned to better hone the power. Mombi, he assumed, used the siphoned magic for the pumpkins, but he would put it to much better use.

Probably to grow some shitty pumpkins too, though.

Whatever.

"I'm going to take a bath," he told Ozma.

She flicked a look at him before eying the water as if she expected something terrible to surface. "Okay..."

He quickly shed his clothes and stepped into the water, completely unfazed by his nudity. The thought of Ozma seeing him bare didn't cross his mind until after the cool water lapped over his skin. It sent a shiver up his spine, goosebumps rising, and he dipped beneath the surface, eyes closed. *My lake.* He scrubbed himself, removing the layers of sweat and dirt, while his body got used to the temperature.

A pair of hands grabbed his arm and for a brief moment, horror filled Jack. Had he not really killed the undine? But then wisps of blonde hair caught his attention, floating around Ozma like a halo. Jack let out a relieved breath and followed the bubbles to the surface.

"What?" he gasped, wiping the water from his eyes.

"You were down there for a long time," Ozma said. "I thought maybe you were in trouble."

Jack's eyes caught on her bare arms skimming the water's

surface and he smirked. "So concerned that you took off your dress first?"

She scowled. "I got in to bathe since I was interrupted last time, *then* thought you needed help."

"Right."

Ozma splashed at him. "You're welcome."

Jack laughed—a real laugh. His first in two years. He flicked water back at her. She gasped and flung an even bigger splash at him. Again and again, until the entire surface of the lake rippled around them and they were both winded, their chests heaving. The swells at the tops of her breasts drew his attention. Ozma stopped first, ducking beneath the water—*cheater!*—and waited for Jack to cease before reemerging. Grateful for her quiet surrender, he took only seconds to stop.

"You know," Jack started once the lake had calmed again, "I used to come here with Tip frequently." He cast an unsure glance at Ozma, worried she wouldn't want to hear about his relationship with her brother.

Ozma's eyes flashed with interest, but she quickly lowered her gaze. The hair that had come loose from her braids clung to the sides of her face, making her appear younger. "Since you both needed to bathe, I'm not surprised."

"We didn't just come here for that."

Ozma blushed. It was a good color on her—he wanted to see more of it.

"We also came," Jack continued, "to give ourselves a moment to breathe." She stared at him wordlessly as a crease formed between her brows. "It was too far for Mombi to walk, so we had to fill a tub for her instead. Which was fucking backbreaking work, but it was worth it because we could really be ourselves here. Talk about anything, dream about escaping, kiss…" *Fuck each other senseless.* He paused to see if the information made her uncomfortable, but she simply watched him as if waiting for him to continue.

"Tell me about him," Ozma said when he remained silent,

lowering herself so the water skimmed her bottom lip.

Jack ran a hand through his hair. It twisted his insides to think of Tip in detail, but it also hurt not to. "As I'm sure you know from your time in the mirror, we grew up here together. He was all I had, and I was all he had, too. Except, I could sometimes leave under Mombi's control, so I suppose he had it worse than me.

"Still, he didn't let it bring him down much. Tip always had a smile for me, always told me not to worry. His laugh was like the sun and his eyes were even brighter. Tip was the purest soul I've ever met—not that I've met many—and I didn't deserve him."

Could I sound more like a sap? But, damn me, it's fucking true.

Jack's gaze locked on the ripples widening along the surface of the water as he willed away his pain. He missed everything about Tip. The way he hummed while they worked the field and how he tugged on his ear when he was nervous. When his jealousy tinged his cheeks pink. The softness of his hair, the tingling sensation Tip's touch put in Jack's chest, and the silly faces he would carve into pumpkins.

"It must've taken you a long time to get over him," Ozma said with a question in her tone.

Jack huffed. "I've never gotten over him. Believe me, it would be better if I could."

She watched him carefully. "But the other day—"

"A prostitute from town," Jack said quickly, and winced. *Great thinking, asshole. Dig yourself a deeper hole, why don't you?* Not that Ozma should care. "That doesn't sound good, I know, and the next part is even worse. But I... Well, I fuck whores that look like Tip to bury my pain. And, before you ask, no, it doesn't make me feel better. It makes me feel worse, in fact."

"Then why keep doing it?" she asked, her eyes like saucers.

"Why?" He took a deep breath and searched his mind for the answer. "I don't know. Maybe I hope that, if I keep trying, one day it *will* work. That some of my pain will lessen for longer than it takes for pleasure to come and go."

Ozma swam forward slowly, as if she were afraid he would flee, and smoothed a lock of wet hair from his face. "You're wrong."

Fucking hell—her eyes were just *like Tip's.* He wanted to lose himself in her gaze. Lose himself in other parts of her too. It had been ages since he'd felt the warmth of a female, and he couldn't help feeling drawn to her. But she was Tip's sister. If he were going to screw his way through Loland to forget Tip, he certainly couldn't entertain the idea of adding Tip's sister to the mix. And yet…

"Wrong about what?" he croaked.

"I can tell how much you still love Tip after all this time. If that doesn't prove your devotion, nothing would."

"I never claimed otherwise, so what am I wrong about?"

Ozma swam backward toward the shore. "You deserved him."

Jack felt frozen in the water as she reached the edge of the lake and walked, naked, into the tall grass. The twitch in his cock told him *she* was wrong. Lusting after Tip's sister made him extremely unworthy, but the pang in his chest was harder. A crack formed and tears stung Jack's eyes. He quickly ducked beneath the surface again to wash them away.

Chapter Eleven

Ozma

Ozma squeezed the water from her hair as she walked back toward the farm with a happy—albeit confused—heart. Jack still loved her... Or no, it was *Tip* that he still loved. It didn't matter, because it was her either way. And there had been a reason he'd had the male in his hut—a prostitute—who had looked like Tip. Ozma hadn't taken the time to study the male's face, or similarities, since she'd been too focused on Jack, sweat-slicked and thrusting inside another. Perhaps that was why there'd been so many clients at the brothel where she'd stopped with Reva when they journeyed. *Loneliness.* She could understand Jack feeling that way, even if she hated what he was doing to fill a void.

It didn't mean anything that Ozma was Tip because she'd changed so much over the last two years that she was hardly the same fae inside. She hadn't even confessed to Jack who her parents really were, who *she* was. Not *only* Ozma. Not *only* a female who had responsibilities. All she'd been focused on before was her love for Jack, not the pressure that her royal status would put on him.

Fisting her hands, Ozma walked inside Mombi's hut. Jack's magic was beautiful, the way he could get things to grow, make the grass appear like it was dancing, even when going in for a kill. How could Mombi have done this to him? To her? She wanted to stab the witch in the heart over and over again.

Now that Jack was no longer in and out of sleep, Ozma needed to formulate a plan and gather any spells she could from Mombi's so she could head to Orkland for the Wizard. Blowing out a breath, she went into Mombi's room and started collecting the spell books. Piling as many tomes as she could in her arms, Ozma took them across the patch and loaded the books into the wagon. After all the books were out of the hut, Ozma grabbed the jars of ingredients, until she was certain she'd plucked away everything she could possibly use.

Once she returned to the sitting room, she gathered candles, created from goblin skin, and lit one, then another and another. She put a flame to the remaining candles in Mombi's room before knocking them, one by one, to the bed, then to the floor with a thump. Black and orange fire spread its way across the blankets, the filthy walls. As it engulfed the room, Ozma set flames to the curtains in the sitting room, watching as they crawled throughout, going past the spot where she'd discovered her true self.

Ozma remained in the middle of the sitting room, studying herself in the mirror, the bright orange, black, and gray around her, until the heat became too much against her skin, the smoke too heavy for her lungs. As she turned to leave, the door swung open with a *crack*.

"What in the ever-loving fuck are you doing?" Jack shouted. He motioned his hand back and forth through the smoke as he hurried toward her. Before she could say anything, he lifted her from the floor and cradled her against his chest, then rushed outside.

Ozma couldn't contain her emotions anymore. The tears came, her sobs echoed throughout the patch. "Put me down!

Stop trying to save me when I can save my own damn self! For once."

"Okay," he breathed, setting Ozma down and cradling her face, his gaze latching onto hers. "Okay. But what am I supposed to think when you're standing in the middle of the hut, watching it burn around you?"

"Ask me if I need help before swooping in," she whispered, not being able to shift her eyes from his hazel irises.

"*Do* you need help?" he asked, lifting a brow.

She did. Jack had magic, and she didn't. Even if he hadn't had any magic at all, she still needed him on this journey.

"Will you come with me to kill the Wizard in Orkland?" she asked softly, as his hands released her face. "It wasn't only Mombi who sent me away to the dark place. It was him, and if he doesn't die, then Reva and everyone else will be in danger." Ozma paused, taking in a deep breath. "I do have magic, but I learned from Mombi's spell books that the Wizard's been absorbing it with the silver slippers. He must have somehow gotten them from Thelia when she left Oz."

Jack stared at her, cocking his head like he didn't fully understand. Behind them, the crackles of Mombi's burning home sounded, the smoke curling into the air, the flames ripping through the hut to the outer layers.

"Thelia is Dorothy, remember?" she pointed out. "Anyway, I promised Reva that once I defeated the Wizard I would meet her back in the Emerald City. You don't know Reva—if I don't go there, she'll come looking for me. But I understand if you choose not to go." She would just have to hope that the spells from Mombi's books would be enough.

"If you had magic, I'm assuming Tip did too, and Mombi did the same thing to all of us."

Ozma slowly nodded. *Truth.*

"You're not telling me something." Jack took a step closer. "I still feel like you're leaving out information."

"Do you want to come or not?" There were some things that

Jack still didn't know the truth about, but she wasn't going to tell him. One day he would learn she was a queen, but she was too far into the lie to tell him that she was Tip.

"Yes," he finally said. "I'll come with you."

"You do know you're free now, though," she whispered. "Free, Jack. Just because I'm asking you to come doesn't mean you have to. Mombi's dead—you aren't bound to do anything you don't want to."

"I was never very good at taking orders." He smirked. "From the bitch, anyway."

Ozma turned from that face she yearned to touch and walked away from him, toward the wagon.

"When did Mombi get a wagon?" As she tugged open the door and lifted one of the spell books, Jack stopped at the opening with his arms crossed.

"After Tip died, she sent me out of the barrier to collect one. She used it for the last couple of years when she journeyed out more by herself." He watched her flip through two of the tomes before asking, "Are you going to pass one over or hoard them all?"

She picked up a tattered sickly-green one and tossed it at Jack. He stepped out of the way and the book landed on the ground with a plop.

"You were supposed to catch it." She rolled her eyes and threw him another.

He easily caught it then picked up the one from the ground. Licking a finger, he turned a few pages before meeting her gaze. "What am I looking for here, Blossom?"

"Just anything that might help us." Ozma bit the inside of her cheek—nothing so far appeared useful.

"I'm pretty sure making fae lust after pumpkin pie isn't going to save anyone." He crawled into the wagon and sat across from her.

Ozma let out a huff and sifted through more pages. Raising the dead, putting someone under the spellcaster's command, shifting someone into an animal. She tore out those pages and set them aside to stick in her satchel. The rest of the books didn't seem like they would be worth anything, unless she wanted to rot herself from the inside out while using dark magic or cheat fae at the market.

The note from before, about Lurline's baby being stolen, caught her attention again when she thumbed through its book one more time. Something in her didn't want to put it back in between the pages, so she stuffed the note inside her bag too.

The night started to darken and Ozma hadn't realized so much time had passed. She peeked out at the twinkling sky, at Mombi's smoldering, collapsed hut across the field, and stretched her arms. When a book hit the wagon floor with a *thump*, her gaze darted to Jack.

"How about we get some rest and head out in the morning?" he asked.

Even though she'd been up for most of the night, watching over Jack, she wasn't tired enough to sleep. "Go ahead. I'm going to stay out here a little longer."

"All right." Jack hopped out of the wagon and walked off toward his hut, leaving Ozma to wonder if she'd said something wrong.

Shrugging off the odd feeling, she slipped out of the wagon, trekking over vines and around the large pumpkins Jack had created with his magic the night before. In the middle of the pumpkin patch, she lay down on the grass, letting the fruit surround her, and the stars hover above. This was something she'd always liked to do—count the stars, connect them with an imaginary line to make shapes, while hoping to one day escape the patch.

Footsteps sounded and she sat up, spotting Jack with a lantern and a bowl of something in his hand.

"Here," he said, giving her the bowl filled with pumpkin-seed brittle and two plums. "You know, Tip used to like lounging in the middle of the field at night too."

I know. "Really?"

"Yeah," he said quietly.

"Hmm." She took a piece of brittle and bit into it, surveying the shifting silhouettes of trees in the dark. Jack sank down beside Ozma, the pumpkins practically cocooning them closer together so that his thigh brushed hers and his pinky finger grazed her wrist. Neither spoke as they both gazed up at the sky.

Her heart thumped, harder, *harder*, her chest tightening at his nearness, his scent. She couldn't breathe, her body aching as a warmth spread through her. There were times she couldn't control herself as Tip, just as she couldn't now. Seized by her old reckless habit of needing to kiss him, she grabbed his face and pressed her lips to his. Soft. His mouth was always soft, perfect.

There wasn't any hesitation as Jack kissed her back, urgent, spreading her lips with his tongue. He gripped her by the waist and lifted her with one easy swoop into his lap, her legs cradling his hips. Her center was right against his hard length, and a moan escaped her mouth as emotions rushed through her body, like a magical tornado taking down the entire world. It had never felt like this—this sensitive, this *good*, as he moved her hips forward, again and again. And his cock wasn't even in her yet. Her tongue licked and danced with his as she ran her hands in his hair, grasping, tugging it. He released a low groan, and she responded by drawing him even closer. She couldn't stop kissing him, that familiar taste, those movements, that body she needed to see bare again like earlier at the lake, that—

"Tip," Jack murmured, sucking and nipping at her bottom lip.

Ozma froze, then leapt from his lap. What was she doing? She'd said she would let him be free and then she'd done this. And he'd called her Tip… Who she *was*, but he didn't know that.

Jack blinked, his mouth parting, seeming to be at a loss for words as he stared at her. "Ozma," he finally said, as if that would make everything better.

"It's fine." Ozma took a swallow, tugging at her ear. "I've

gotta go to sleep. See you in the morning, Jack."

She didn't want to hear his apologies as she whirled around and hurried across the patch to his hut. Jack didn't chase after her—she was sure he was hating himself for calling her the wrong name and thinking he'd kissed Tip's sister.

Why had she made up this ridiculous lie?

Chapter Twelve

Jack

Jack sat among the pumpkins, watching Ozma hurry away from him, with the taste of her still on his lips, the roof of his mouth, his tongue. *What the hell just happened?*

She'd kissed him.

She kissed me.

He hadn't initiated anything, though he'd wanted to. He knew damn well his cock had wanted to. But he'd tried to behave. Then her lips touched his and that was it—he didn't give a flying fuck anymore. He wanted to take and take and take until Ozma had nothing left to give.

And then she ran. Because he'd, stupidly, called her Tip. *Fuck me.* She tasted just like him though. Savory and just a little bit sweet. Her tongue stroked his, her hands waking every inch of skin she touched. For the briefest moment, it had made him forget that it was Tip's sister he was kissing.

Jack lay back and dragged a hand over his face. Maybe it was for the best. Nothing could truly happen between them while he was still so in love with Tip, and yet... He closed his eyes and unapologetically replayed the kiss anyway. The first press of her warm lips, the way her tongue danced with his, how they seemed to melt together. It felt like they'd kissed a thousand times before.

She tugged her ear.

Jack's eyes flew open at the unbidden thought. Ozma … tugged her ear. His pulse raced. Tip did that—exactly like that. Two quick pulls followed by a longer one. And she knew the way to the lake without hesitation. That was impossible if she'd spent her life inside a mirror, and then the dark place. The look of betrayal on her face when she'd seen him with the prostitute…

Mombi's dark magic could do just about anything.

No… It wasn't possible, was it? Could Ozma be Tip? Would she admit it if he confronted her? If it were true and she wanted him to know, she would've told him. Right? He ran his thumb over his bottom lip. *No.* Ozma was a liar. Which meant Tip was a liar. But Tip *never* lied, at least not to him. The thought of Tip hiding a truth so large left him feeling cold inside. There was only one way forward—get Ozma to admit the truth. And, to do that, he would need to arm himself with proof.

Jack leapt up from the ground and sprinted to the wagon. With a quick glance toward his hut to make sure Ozma wouldn't see him, he slipped inside, leaving the painted door open a crack to use the moonlight. The scent of dried herbs with a hint of sweat assaulted his senses.

"What did you take from Mombi's hut, Blossom?" he asked aloud.

Flipping through each book, he found nothing surprising. Dark magic spells for this, dark magic potions for that. But then he glanced at Ozma's satchel, still resting inside the wagon, practically calling to him. He shouldn't. *He should.* With hurried motions, he unlatched the flap and collected a few of the notes resting inside. Spells… Then a handwritten note.

Steal the child growing in Lurline's belly.
Use magic to alter the child's identity.

Find silver slippers to draw magic from the child.
Create immortality

"What the fuck?" he whispered. Was this talking about Tip—Ozma… Which identity was true? And who was Lurline? The slippers and the immortality had to be regarding the Wizard, just as Ozma explained before. Altering the child's identity would explain Ozma being Tip too.

"What are you doing?" Ozma asked. She stood in the open door with a bundle of blankets, staring with wide eyes at the note in Jack's hand.

Jack turned the paper so she could see it. "Why do you have this?"

"In… In case it helps destroy the Wizard."

Liar. Or, if not a lie, then she was holding something back. "Who is the baby?"

Ozma hopped into the wagon, dropped the bundle, and quickly took the note and the other spell pages from Jack's hands. "How should I know? It also isn't polite to go through someone's things." Jack watched in silence as she tucked the page away inside her satchel. "We should get some sleep."

"Right," he said carefully. "Sleep."

There was no way he would be able to shut his mind off tonight, but his body begged him to try. So he followed Ozma back to his hut and nestled down in front of the fireplace so she could take his room again.

Tip.

Ozma.

Mombi and the Wizard…

He mentally tried to piece everything together as his eyelids grew impossibly heavy. None of the pieces fit—not yet. But he wouldn't stop trying until they did.

Sleep did nothing to erase the insane thoughts running through Jack's mind. He hoped it would bring him to his senses. Hoped that it was simply residual exhaustion from what had happened with Mombi that put strange ideas in his head. Ozma was Tip. She couldn't be … but she was. He was almost certain of it. If he could just make her admit it…

Jack sat in a wobbly chair and watched Ozma pick through his paltry shelves for something other than his home-brewed ale, stuffing anything edible into a sack for their journey to Orkland. She moved differently than Tip had. Smoother and less awkward. And she didn't need to stand on her toes to reach the higher shelves. Could Mombi adjust a fae's height? He scowled. If she could change everything else about someone, was that even really a question?

"If I didn't know any better, I'd say you were a drunkard." Ozma turned toward him and froze. "What's with that look?"

Jack rapped his fingers on the tabletop. "If you didn't know any better?" She *would* know. Better than anyone else.

"I'm not judging you. Living with Mombi almost required a muddled head," she said with a shrug.

"But why *would* you know any better? Why wouldn't you assume I *am* a drunkard?" Ozma wouldn't know if he drank once a year or every night if she'd been in Mombi's mirror. *Tip* would've known that Jack only drank on the really hard days, but that wasn't exactly true anymore. Every day was a hard day since Tip had died.

Or didn't *die.*

Was Tip stuck as Ozma, or was this her true form? Any curse Mombi placed on her should've broken when she died. Unless dark magic was used… So had Tip always been Ozma? The note mentioned altering a child's identity, so the infant would have had to be born as Ozma. He chewed his bottom lip.

What a mind fuck.

"I don't understand." Ozma's brows knitted together. "Are you trying to tell me that you *are* a drunkard? Sorry, but you need a clear head on this journey. All the jars stay."

Jack swallowed a frustrated scream. Was she really this good at acting? He already knew she was a liar, but this was extreme. Why wouldn't she tell him if she'd been Tip?

Because she caught you with your dick in someone else.

Shit.

Orkland was a two-day journey—one by land, another by boat—so Jack would have to pay close attention to gather proof. Ozma would slip up again like she had when she'd tugged her ear. "I don't need to bring any," he said as casually as possible.

Maybe one or two…

No.

He would sober his sorry ass up on this trip if it was the last thing he did. Ozma was a sly one—getting the truth would require him to have all his wits about him.

"Then I'm ready if you are," Ozma said, hefting the sack of food over her shoulder.

Jack reached out, took the heavy bag from her, and swept an arm toward the door. "After you."

He followed her from his hut, then took one final look around the small, worn shelter. Would he ever be back? It was the only home he'd known, so even though he'd been forced to live there, leaving felt bittersweet. Every moment he'd had with Tip had been on this farm. His eyes narrowed. But, apparently, they could keep making memories together—as Jack and Ozma. The idea of having more time together sent prickles of warmth through him, but he shut it down quickly.

He had to be *right* before he allowed hope to settle in.

After depositing the sack of food in the back of the wagon, Ozma whistled. The stag trotted from the woods and stood calmly as she hitched him up. Jack took note of her sureness as she connected the straps properly—something else she wouldn't have learned inside the mirror. But Tip would've known. As very small younglings, they'd had a wretched, swayback mare to help turn the soil for a few years before it dropped dead.

Jack climbed up beside Ozma to begin their journey, gnawing his bottom lip. He let her navigate the way to the sea. The forest he knew so well gave way to sparser trees with tall, umbrella-like leaves, and the dirt road lightened to white clay. Homes were made from brick with thatched roofs. Instead of lush grass, it grew tall and wispy with tiny tufts at the top of each blade.

Every turn Ozma made was done with a sureness he couldn't begin to grasp. If she was in the mirror, and then some dark place, she would have no idea where to go. He already knew the mirror was a lie because she walked around like she owned every inch of the farm, but what about the dark place?

Pain shot through his chest. If there was no dark place, where had Ozma been the last two years? Because Tip wouldn't know his way around Loland either. Not when he'd been stuck on the farm. So, if the dark place was a lie, why had she waited to come back? Was it because of Mombi? Or was it because she hadn't wanted to see Jack? Warmth flooded over him, a mixture of fear and embarrassment. He'd longed for Tip for two years ... but when he'd returned as Ozma, there were only lies. Lies about who she really was. Lies about where she'd been. His mind twisted and twisted around itself, tying complicated knots of nerves.

"Do you want to stop and stretch your legs?" Ozma asked quietly as the sun sank below the tree line, breaking the silence between them.

Jack shook his head.

"And to eat?" Her voice became even more uncertain.

"I'm not hungry," Jack told her coolly.

She swallowed audibly. "We should give the stag a rest, at least. There are a few more hours before we reach the sea."

And how would you know? Jack crossed his arms over his chest. "Maybe we should camp here for the night."

"Here?" Ozma scoured the area. There were plenty of places to steer the wagon off the road. Though the trees wouldn't offer any coverage, they hadn't seen another traveler all day. It seemed safe enough.

"Why not?" he asked. "You can sleep in the back of the wagon." *Not we.*

"Me?" Both her brows lifted. "Where will you sleep?"

"Out here." He motioned to thin woodland. The ground was flat, the dirt dry and packed, with leaves scattered about. It would've been preferrable to sleep inside the wagon, but there was no way he could rest being so close to Ozma.

She hesitated. "We should keep going. There will probably be somewhere nearer to the port so we can catch the first ship to Orkland."

"Why does it have to be the first ship?" he asked in a flat voice. They had no solid plan of attack to defeat the Wizard, which sat uneasy with Jack. Neither of them had fighting skills—at least, that he knew of—and Ozma had no magic. Unless that was a lie too. His magic could grow things, but it was still highly untested. Killing one undine didn't make him battle-ready. It felt more like they'd gotten lucky with Mombi than anything, and the Wizard wasn't one to be messed with. Jack hadn't seen him in two years, but before that the mortal had aged over the time he visited the farm, grown frail and crazed from his fruit addiction. Yet still, he exuded power. The hair on Jack's arms always stood on end when he visited and the sense of unease lingered long after he left.

"I suppose it doesn't," Ozma conceded. "But you want to visit the sea."

Jack quirked a brow. "Do I?" *Keep calm.* The only one who knew about his desire to set eyes on the sea was Tip. "Maybe I hate water."

Ozma blushed and gave him a shy smile as she steered their wagon onto a flat, grassy area beside the road. "I just assumed… Since you've been on the farm your entire life."

Jack studied her carefully, desperate to see some physical sign that Ozma and Tip were the same fae. Nothing. Only those fucking blue eyes he loved so much. "I gave up wanting anything a long time ago."

Ozma's smile fell. "Don't say that."

"Tell me"—he leaned closer and closer, then lifted her chin—"what do you think is left for me, then?"

Her eyes dropped to his mouth as she spoke. "You have your whole life ahead of—"

Jack snorted, releasing her face. "Don't bother, Blossom. Unless you can tell me Tip is still alive…"

Take the bait.

Take. It.

Ozma opened and shut her mouth. "I'll get us something to eat from the back," she said, sounding defeated.

Jack hung his head as she climbed down from the seat beside him. Was he wrong? Was it wishful thinking? He squeezed his eyes shut before they could threaten him with tears. There was no explanation other than Ozma being Tip.

I'm not wrong.

But why was she still lying to him?

Chapter Thirteen

Ozma

Jack had been acting differently toward Ozma the entire day… And it had to be because of the night before, in the patch, beneath the stars. That damn kiss. That beautiful kiss. The kiss she couldn't stop thinking about, even when she'd disappeared into Jack's hut to try and get some sleep. Instead, she'd explored her body—her breasts, the slick folds between her legs, feeling things that were good—but could be even better, when done by another's hands. Then she'd gone outside to check on him and had found him in the wagon, holding that note of Mombi's that she should have burned instead of kept. Luckily, she'd been quick to have an answer about it.

Ozma straightened in the seat of the wagon, shaking off the night before, and focusing on the trees blooming with bright fruits and nuts. The map in her veins lit up, and she knew if they took the shortcut through the forest, they could make it to the sea sooner. Pulling the reins, she steered the stag off the sandy road.

"Where are you going?" Jack asked, grabbing onto her wrist.

"It's faster this way. Trust me." She smiled as he gave her an unsure look. Then Ozma cursed herself because that was the reason Jack was acting funny, not because she'd kissed him. But because he still didn't fully trust her, and he probably thought she'd been trying to seduce him for some nefarious reason. No, that wouldn't be right, because she hadn't asked a thing while she'd been planted against him, feeling every inch and curve of his delicious mouth. Hurriedly, Ozma tucked that down and focused on the clear sky.

As she glanced at him, she inwardly sighed, knowing she should just give him something else. "I know where to go, Jack, because, while I don't have magic, there is something within me that knows where lands and seas are. Like an internal map. Perhaps that is magic, or perhaps it's just a part of me. So that's how I know."

"Oh. We shouldn't get lost then." Jack bit his lip, appearing conflicted, as though he wanted to say something different but held back.

Ozma arched an eyebrow at him. "We certainly won't."

They traveled deeper and deeper into the forest until trees with their tops in the shape of mushrooms covered its entirety. Branches intertwined and curved like snakes, the sun's light dimming and squeezing through the narrow slits from above.

"Listen … Ozma," Jack said, placing his hands behind his neck.

"No more *Blossom*?" she asked, trying to make things light as she tightened her grip on the reins. But something about his tone made her nervous.

He chuckled and snagged a few leaves from a branch, tearing them to small pieces as he spoke, "Oh, you're most definitely sweeter than any flower." Then his expression grew serious, his lips forming a thin line. "I want to apologize for last night. I didn't mean to call you Tip."

So he wanted to discuss that… "It was all my fault anyway." She winced. "I shouldn't have … done that."

"I don't know." Jack smirked.

Ozma furrowed her brow at his response. He didn't know what? Did he want her to do it again? He was tumbling prostitutes and guzzling pumpkin ale as a means to get over Tip. But even if he did see something to desire in her, she needed to keep to her decision and not shackle him with a crown. Still, those lush lips and those long fingers kept drawing her gaze.

The wagon bounced up and jolted to the side as a loud snap echoed. Ozma and Jack lurched forward, the stag grunting while trying to turn before coming to a halt. A sudden shift to the right caused Ozma to slide off the seat, releasing the reins, and clawing at air as her backside hit the ground. She groaned as a sharp ache ran up her spine. Jack almost landed on top of her, but grabbed her and rolled her with him to his back, until she was above him.

"Are you all right?" Jack rasped, lifting her chin. "Did it worsen your wounds from the undine?"

"I'm fine," Ozma lied. Her back still throbbed, but it was slowly dissipating. She searched around to see if anyone had attacked the wagon, but only the stag stood there. "And you?"

"I've been through worse." Jack's smirk returned as he sat them both up with her in his lap. "This reminds me of last night. Your body against mine, your legs cradling my hips." He tugged on a lock of her hair, twirling it around his finger. "Have I told you how much I like the gold?"

Something felt off here. The way he was looking at her, as though he wanted to kiss her right then. "Did you sneak pumpkin ale on the ride, or did you hit your head?" Ozma quickly stood, leaving his heat, and brushed the dirt from her dress. She glanced at the front of their ride, where one of the wheels had fallen off, making the wagon tilt to the right.

"Just lightening the mood." He scanned their means of transportation and walked to a nearby tree where part of the wheel lay broken. "At least we weren't being attacked."

"This is only going to slow us down. Couldn't the wagon have at least made it to the port first?" Perhaps she should have just taken the longer route and stayed on the sandy road. But it would take them longer to turn back now.

"Apparently, the wagon wasn't made for softer terrain." He tapped the closest tree with his knuckles.

Ozma shot Jack a dirty look as she strode toward the stag. He bucked his head and stomped in place. Hot air hit her face from each of his heavy snorts.

"Quit being antsy," Ozma said, reaching out a hand to calm the stag, stroking his soft fur. She looked from the broken wheel to Jack. "You don't have anything to fix it, do you?"

"Yes, I carry huge pristine wheels in my pocket." He patted his pants and shook his head. "Of course not. I wouldn't know how to replace a wagon wheel if I tried. Mombi always used magic to do things like that. She assumed I would have left it loose." A wicked grin spread across his face, stretching his freckles. "Not that I wouldn't have."

Ozma gave him a small smile. She was good at repairing things back then and now, but even if she could change out a wheel, there wasn't one for her to use.

The stag released another annoyed huff.

"All right. All right." She reached for the reins and started to unbuckle the straps from his body. "Now you can be free." There was no reason for the stag to stick around longer than he had to.

"Hold on now." Jack lifted a hand toward the stag. "We can still ride him to the port and not lose any time."

Ozma peered up at the stag, unsure if he would let them ride him, but they could try.

A loud shriek sounded in the distance as she took a step forward. Something like branches cracking reverberated and the stag jerked, barreling off in the direction of the road. Ozma stood frozen beside Jack before yanking out her dagger. He held out his hand, as if prepared to release his magic.

When nothing else came, Jack rolled his eyes. "Or not. Could have at least given us a goodbye first, stag."

She was just glad he'd taken them this far. Blowing out a

breath, Ozma opened the door to the wagon, collected her satchel, and handed Jack his pack. Inside, the wagon was mostly empty, except for the extra fruit they'd brought. Before she and Jack had left that morning, she'd cleared out Mombi's spell books and burned them. No one needed to find those tomes and use that sort of darkness on other fae. No one deserved to go through what she and Jack had.

"Ready?" Ozma asked.

Jack opened his pack and fished out a plum. "Now I am." He bit into the thin skin as they walked deeper into the forest. The mushroom-shaped trees seemed to get shorter, and the trunks wider, the farther they trekked. Dryads—with leaves for ears and bodies covered in thorns and twigs—would poke their heads out, large eyes blinking, then scurry back inside the trees.

"So," Jack finally said when a lavender-winged sprite flew past them. "Is Ozma part of your true name or was it one Mombi gave you? Tip could never feel his true name."

Ozma closed her eyes briefly, recalling how she would say Jack's true name—Jackseith Arel Diosyll—to try and force him to escape Mombi. But Mombi's magic was always too strong for it to work. She thought about her own true name and tapped into it. The one she hadn't known until after she'd met Reva, but it hadn't mattered then, and it didn't now, because she still couldn't draw up magic. *Ozma Emeraldis Dynasia.* Her heart sped up as she silently repeated it over and over. Nothing.

"Yes, it's part of my true name." She shrugged. "I didn't know all of it before, not until the dark place."

"I think I like Blossom better." He pressed a red flower into her hair that he'd taken from a small patch on the forest floor.

She left it there, her heart speeding up from how gentle his movement had been.

Neither spoke for a long while as they skirted around trunks and dodged vines lined with sharp spikes.

In the distance, there were several huge trees, forming a half-circle, stretching into the sky, taller and wider than she'd ever seen. Gnarled branches bloomed from the tops and sides of the charcoal-colored trunks. Dark blue leaves grew across the limbs while others decorated the ground where they'd fallen. Long brown vines with scarlet leaves dangled over the large openings—similar to a cave entrance—at the front of each trunk.

Ozma glanced up at the sky, noticing it would be dark soon. She didn't know how safe it would be staying the night here, but they would have to make do. Besides, she didn't think Jack would be able to handle sleeping at the top of a tree like she could. The wagon would have been ideal, but that was far behind them now.

"You want to stop there for the night?" Ozma pointed to the tree in the middle. "Or go farther and hope we find something better."

Jack squinted as he lifted his chin, seeming to search around the trunks.

Ozma smiled, latched onto a shorter tree beside her, and quickly scaled her way up until she was near the branches at the top.

"You're quite fast at that," Jack called up to her. "Even in a dress."

In the dark place, a dress was all she'd had to wear after she'd abandoned her old clothing, so she'd grown used to it, rather liking the loose fit more than trousers.

"Two years with Reva," she shouted down, then studied the surrounding trees and past them into the distance. "I can't really see anything. Only foliage and more foliage."

After Ozma touched ground again, she and Jack gathered twigs and dried leaves to start a fire outside, near where they were staying, to give them light without burning the whole tree down. They set the things on the ground to start the fire later, then headed inside the large trunk in the middle. Ozma pushed aside the vines at the entrance, allowing Jack to enter the dark space first. A smoky smell struck her nose as she stepped next to Jack.

From the outside, a small bit of light entered, making

shadows dance along the wall. Jack moved forward, examining the trunk's walls. Ozma glanced down just as his foot was about to step into nothingness.

"Jack!" She rushed to grab his arm and yank him back. But it was too late—his body fell forward, taking her with him.

A squeak escaped her mouth at the same time he shouted, "Fuck!" Her stomach was somewhere down in her knees and she couldn't get a scream out.

Above them, the opening fell farther and farther away. Small bugs with glowing blue bodies scurried along the dark walls, the only light guiding their way as they continued their descent.

Into the darkness below.

Chapter Fourteen

Jack

Down, down, down, they fell.

Jack couldn't pull in air. Couldn't cry out another curse. *Fuck!* Twisting, he managed to hug Ozma to his chest, his back to whatever fate lay beneath them as the blue glow of bugs blurred around them. His stomach rose, the plum he ate earlier threatening to make a reappearance. All he could do was hold onto Ozma. Hold on and hope there was a soft landing.

Because if there wasn't, they were dead.

Pain seared across Jack's back. A breath was torn from him, only to be met with a mouthful of freezing cold water. Too stunned by the razor-sharp sting and frigid temperature, he didn't immediately try to surface as the pool of water swallowed him.

Them.

His grip on Ozma had become steel—a reflex against the shock. It was her struggling against him in an attempt to swim that finally snapped him out of it. With a powerful kick, Jack catapulted them upward until they found the surface. They both gasped, the sound echoing off the cavernous stone walls. Specks of blue light reflected off the water's rippling surface and the sound of sloshing water filled his ears.

"Are you okay?" Jack choked out.

Ozma nodded, teeth chattering. The blue light dancing on her face gave her an ethereal appearance. "You?"

"I'll live." Assuming there was somewhere to exit the water. If not, they would quickly exhaust themselves swimming and drown. His back hurt so tremendously from slapping the surface of the pool that he couldn't inhale deeply. He needed a place to lie down for a moment and collect himself.

Jack scanned the area, more than grateful for the glow of the bugs. They cast everything in breathtaking wonder. If it weren't for their situation, Jack would've loved to gaze up at them in awe all night long. But they *were* in a situation. A fucking bad one.

Smooth rock curved up to the hole they'd fallen from. It was impossible to tell how far they'd tumbled, but far enough that the opening seemed no larger than an average pumpkin. Vines hung around the edges like fringe. There was no climbing back up, even if the walls offered footholds.

"Fuck," he mumbled. "Fuck. *Fuck*."

"There," Ozma rasped, pointing. "Shore."

Jack's eyes found what she meant, but he hardly considered it a *shore*. A slab of stone stuck out from the wall, large enough for perhaps a dozen fae to sit comfortably, but there was no obvious exit. "There's—" His words caught when he found the spot beside him empty. Heart stumbling over itself, his eyes quickly landed on a blonde head already gliding toward it.

A relieved sigh fell from his chest as he started after her. He swam as fast as he could with the ache radiating through him. It took more out of him than he would admit aloud as he caught up to Ozma at the rock. Jack heaved himself over the ledge first. The stone was warm—too warm considering the cold water and lack of sunlight—but he wasn't about to complain. Taking Ozma's hand, he hauled her up beside him and collapsed on his stomach.

"Jack?" Ozma touched his back and a hiss escaped from between his teeth. "You said you were okay…"

He grunted. "I said I'd live."

"Let me see." Ozma began sliding his shirt up his back.

"Blossom," he said, rolling slightly away, "relax. Let me catch my breath, then we'll look for a way out of here."

She sat back, releasing his shirt, and exhaled loudly. "You catch your breath while *I* find a way out."

"Sure," he said, too tired to argue, and closed his eyes.

A few minutes of careful breathing and Jack felt slightly less winded. He lifted his head, rested his chin on his folded hands, and watched Ozma flip through her satchel then scour the cave for an exit. The fabric of her dress clung to her curves in a way that made him want to touch her—if only moving didn't hurt as much as it did. The kiss, the feel of her body last night, only made the desire worse.

"We're trapped," Ozma finally declared. She spun on her heel and looked at him with fear in her eyes. "There's no way out of here."

"There's always a way," Jack told her. He wouldn't let them die in this place. Too many unseen things were left on his and Tip's list to perish now.

She chewed on her bottom lip and peered up at the opening. "If I had my wings…"

"Wait—what?" He winced as pain prickled worse with his stunned shout. "Wings?"

Ozma pursed her lips, not meeting his gaze. "Mombi cut them off with her magic. The scar on my back…"

Jack remembered the scar. It was large enough for him to see from a distance that night he'd followed her to the lake. "I'm sorry," he whispered. The words seemed louder with the way they echoed through the cavern—or perhaps it was only because his mind was reeling. First, she had a map inside her, and now she had severed wings.

"Don't be." Ozma returned to kneel at Jack's side. "I'll get them back once we find the silver slippers."

If they got them, though Jack admired her tenacity.

"Jack?"

At her nervous tone, he turned his head so he could study her better. "What?"

"We should get out of these wet clothes so they can dry. Don't—" She said when he grinned. "Don't make comments and *don't* peek."

"Fine." He sighed and pushed himself up. The rock would dry their clothes quickly, and they would warm faster if they shared body heat—skin-to-skin, preferably. There was a blanket in his pack they could spread out and— "Shit!"

Ozma jumped at his sudden shout. "What?"

"My pack! It's gone!" He was on his feet in less than a second, looking all over for it but finding only Ozma's satchel. His gaze traveled across the water's surface. "I must've dropped it when we fell."

"Did you have anything important in it?"

Jack raked his hands through his hair. "Food, a blanket, and a…" Grief burned through his chest. "Yes. There was something important in there." He could remember the day he'd gotten Tip's final gift like it was yesterday.

Tip snuck across Jack's hut in an untucked white shirt and pants two sizes too big without a belt. He'd been pressed up against Jack's side only moments ago, stealing a little extra time together before they had to part ways. Tip must've thought Jack was asleep because he'd slipped so carefully from his embrace, but if the creak in the bed hadn't given Tip away, the door would've.

Jack watched him through the open bedroom, his curiosity growing as he forced his expression to remain blank. Why are you sneaking about? *Tip didn't have a devious bone in his body and Jack had no secrets, so it didn't set off any alarms when he heard Tip lift a loose floorboard near the fireplace. Jack kept all his important things there—not that he had many. A few stolen coins and a book of short stories he'd found discarded in the woods.*

Tip was welcome to any of it. They'd read the book together too many times to count, traveling across Oz through the eyes of a fictional hero, and Tip had no use for coins. Not when he was never allowed to leave the farm. Regardless, Jack knew Tip wouldn't take anything without asking.

Tip shuffled about with something and settled the wood back in place with a soft thunk. *Jack closed his eyes and pretended to be asleep as Tip made his way back to the bedroom. The mattress dipped when he climbed onto the edge of it.*

"Jack," Tip whispered. "Wake up."

Jack cracked his eyes and pretended to yawn. "What time is it?"

"Mombi's not looking for us yet," Tip said in a rush. Pink tinged his cheeks and he tugged nervously on his ear. "I… I made you something."

Jack shifted up onto his elbows. Tip was always bringing him little presents that he thought Jack would like to see. An extra-large pine nut or an especially colorful leaf—things no one outside of Mombi's barrier would think twice about. But Tip had never made *him something. "Oh?"*

"It's not very good," Tip continued. "I've been working on it at night after Mombi falls asleep, but—"

"Give it to me," Jack interrupted. Whatever it was, however poorly crafted, he already loved it. Because he loved Tip.

Tip set a rectangular, cloth-covered present into his hand and fidgeted nervously.

Jack smiled at him and moved the fabric away to reveal a small house made of sticks, tied together with twine. Each stick had been snapped off at almost the same length and a pitched roof hung low over the sides. The front door swung in and out with the pull of a pebble. Perfectly imperfect, like most pumpkins in the patch. But better. Because Tip had made it. For him.

"It's … our house," Tip mumbled nervously. "Or what our house would be if we weren't trapped here. Something like that, anyway."

"It's wonderful." Jack beamed at Tip. "I love it."

His blush deepened. "You don't have to say that just because I made it."

Jack clutched the house in one hand and wrapped the other around the back of Tip's neck. "I'm not." He pulled Tip in for a gentle kiss.

Tip smiled against Jack's mouth. Bliss filled Jack's heart at the sensation. In the whole, wide, cruel world, his only shining light was that they'd found each other. That they could make each other so happy without trying. Jack knew he could search a thousand years for another soul like Tip's and never find it.

"Thank you," Jack whispered.

Tip slid a finger along Jack's jaw. "Anything for you."

"I'm sorry, Jack," Ozma said with a hand on his arm, pulling him out of his memory. "We can see if it's at the bottom of the water, if you want."

"No." He swallowed the lump in his throat. Judging by the distance they'd fallen, and the fact that they hadn't hit the bottom of the water, it was too deep and too dark to dive all the way down. And besides, it likely would've broken in his bag. Even broken, he would've treasured it. "We'll never find it."

Ozma hesitated. "What was it? The important thing."

"My seeds," he lied. There *were* pumpkin seeds in his bag so he could potentially begin a new life, but he didn't care about those. He wanted his house. The one he and Tip—*Ozma*—would share a lifetime in once they had the chance. But with her lies, that house felt just as lost as the one in his bag. He forced a small smile and a shrug. "It doesn't matter. I'll find something else to grow."

Ozma nodded and tugged up the skirt of her dress, exposing her legs, when she caught him staring. "Do you mind?"

Jack's gaze traveled over Ozma, which earned him a scowl. He chuckled, keenly aware of the fact that he'd seen her naked already, and faced the opposite direction to undress himself. "Feel free to peek at me all you want," he said with a laugh. When Ozma didn't scold him like he expected, he started to glance back then stopped.

"Jack…" Her voice came out annoyed but he could hear something else there too. Desire?

She was able to see him in all his glory. Jack felt her eyes roaming his strong back, his firm ass, and his broad shoulders. Unashamed as he was, he wanted her to look. Wanted her to see more.

She's lying to you, he reminded himself. *She's Tip and she's lying.*

But it didn't stop his body from reveling in the fact that she was clearly still attracted to him.

When a freezing hand landed on his upper back, he yelped both from the temperature and the pressure against his raw skin. "Have mercy, Blossom. You're cold as ice."

"So are you." Her breath was warm on his neck, sending shivers down his spine. "Turn around but keep your eyes on my face. We'll warm each other up—*not like that,*" she added before he could make an innuendo. "Just … snuggling."

"I can do that," he said in a raspy voice. Though another part of his body was much less certain.

Chapter Fifteen

Ozma

Snuggling? *Snuggling*? Why had Ozma said that word? Gooseflesh covered her from head to toe, and her teeth chattered with a rhythmic pattern of their own. Jack's were doing the same, his hazel eyes glowing beneath the bugs' blue illumination.

Ozma had never been this cold in her life. Not in the dark place during the freezing nights, not when winter winds blew across the pumpkin patch while she'd worked alongside Jack.

She studied Jack for a moment and peered down at his chest, his stomach, his length, even though she'd told him not to look at her. Jerking her head up, she met Jack's gaze again.

With a smile, he held his arms open as he settled on the ground. "You coming or not, Blossom? I'd suggest hurrying up unless you want us to die down here."

Ozma wondered if anyone else had fallen in this hidden pit of a place. There weren't any skeletons in sight, but that didn't mean there weren't any dead below the surface of the water. A shiver rolled through her, not from the thought, but the coldness.

Taking a deep swallow, Ozma lay down and shifted closer to Jack. Closer. Closer. She didn't even know why she'd overreacted with him about her body—he'd seen her bare at the lake. Anyone else who saw her naked, she wouldn't have cared about, yet this was Jack. Reva had seen her in a state of undress all the time when they'd bathed in murky lakes. But Reva hadn't known Ozma before, hadn't laid her eyes on every inch of her old body, to which she could compare things.

"You're taking too long." Jack wrapped his arm around Ozma and drew her the rest of the way to him. "I'm practically dead already."

Neither said a word as he held her close, his chest to her breasts, his calloused hands pressing into her back, his forehead touching hers. Heat spread through her entire body as he rubbed soothing circles up the length of her spine. Her teeth slowly stopped chattering.

The bugs' light seemed to have grown brighter, their steady soft glow shining across the walls. It was like starlight. If only there were a shooting star that she could wish upon to get them out of here. But in that moment, she didn't want to be anywhere else, only in Jack's comforting arms.

"How's your back?" Ozma asked, not wanting to put too much pressure on it as she moved her hands to his neck.

"Perfectly fine," Jack said. The hit to the water had rattled her entire body, stealing her breath for moments.

"If it changes, let me know."

"Careful. I might think you truly care about me."

Ozma felt her face grow hot. "You wish."

He chuckled then, and it was the same musical sound that he only shared when they'd been alone in the past. She couldn't help but smile in return because she loved that laugh.

They both stayed quiet, their breaths increasing. The expression on his face was much better than the somber one he'd held when he'd discovered his pack was long gone. She could dive into the water to search for it, but Jack had been right. There was no way they would be able to locate it, not with how dark the lake was or however deep it went. Her satchel was wet, but everything in there was still intact when she'd checked, including the ink on Mombi's spells.

Their fruit wouldn't last forever though. With no apparent way out, except for the hole practically a sky's distance away, she didn't know what they could try in the morning to escape.

All around her, the bugs' light seemed to lessen, making the area dim, slowly descending into what she feared would be darkness. Every time the world eclipsed of color, she thought about the dark place. She wondered if she died, would she somehow be sent back there again. Her heart beat harder against her ribcage, slamming into Jack's chest.

"Hey"—Jack shook her shoulders—"are you all right?"

"I don't know. It's hard being in the dark sometimes." Ozma's chest heaved as she stared at the fading blue color. She sighed in relief because it hadn't eclipsed completely, but it still unnerved her that it could.

He ran a hand over her damp hair. "Do you want to talk about it?"

"You already know Reva and I constantly ran from things." She bit the inside of her cheek and listened to the slight movement of the water beside them.

"But you never mentioned if you'd been hurt while there," Jack said softly.

Perhaps it would help for her to talk about her experience more instead of keeping such a tight hold on it. After Thelia had pulled them out of the darkness with her magic, Ozma hadn't been able to think about how she truly felt. There had been too many important tasks that needed to get done, beginning with her short journey with Reva before parting ways.

"At first, yes. Mostly scratches and cuts, but I was also bitten a few times. That's when Reva taught me how to climb trees quickly. Up in the branches, I could steer creatures away from Reva. Other times, she would do the same for me."

"I'm glad you had someone there with you." His gaze connected with hers, as they lay on the ground on their sides, and the edges of his lips tilted upward. "Your eyes are even brighter under this light. I like them."

Ozma frowned. "Because they remind you of Tip?"

"No," he drawled. "because they're *yours*."

Before she could speak, he placed that finger over her lips and continued, "It's not just your eyes I like." His hand drifted into her hair. "The color of your hair I *like*, your blossom scent I *like*, your height I *like*, the way your body arches into mine I *like*. Do you want me to go on?"

Her heart pounded faster than it had this whole time, even more so than when she'd been falling down the hole.

"Have you … *tumbled* anyone before?" Jack cleared his throat as if he were hesitant to ask. He'd never used that term when talking about sex—only she had.

"No, I've never *fucked* anyone." *Not in this body anyway.*

"Ah, a beautiful word from a beautiful mouth." Jack's hand slid down her side until it rested at her waist. His nose brushed softly over her lips, his mouth came next, his lips grazing over hers so gently that she wasn't sure if she'd felt them at all.

With a light touch, Jack's other hand moved up to her neck before skimming the curve of her ear. Her body arched into his. For now, there was no way out of this hole, and there was a possibility that they would die down here. If so, then Jack would never get to be free. And neither would she. But perhaps for a while, they could be. She could pretend they weren't trapped, just as she had in the pumpkin patch when Mombi's barrier had kept her hidden.

Jack's mouth hovered over hers, and he lightly licked her bottom lip with the tip of his tongue. "I forgot to mention that I *like* the way you taste."

Done with words, she gripped his hair and kissed him. Slow, too slow, agonizingly slow, but she wanted to taste as much of him as she could before devouring him. A low groan escaped his throat when her tongue entered his mouth, caressing his.

As Jack's lips and tongue lit her body aflame, his cock swelled against her stomach. She wanted to know what it would be like to have his length inside her, how it would feel when she stretched for the first time. Reva had explained to her how tumbling worked as a female, but listening was different than experiencing.

"You're not close enough, Blossom," he rasped, placing her leg around his waist.

"More," she whispered as her center rubbed against his cock.

In a quick swoop, Jack lifted her into his lap and pressed his back against the cave wall. Ozma moaned when his hardness settled perfectly against her core.

As she rolled her hips forward, they both released moans that reverberated around them. Jack's finger glided down the valley between her breasts to slightly above the aching spot between her legs.

"Can I touch you?" he asked, kissing her until both their lips were swollen.

"Please," she murmured, unable to deny whatever he asked right then. "It's been far too long."

Jack froze, halting her from shifting her hips forward again. "What did you say?"

Ozma took a deep swallow, playing back what she'd said, realizing what she'd done wrong.

"You're a liar," Jack said in a low voice. He licked his lower lip and studied her with an intensity that she couldn't begin to describe. "A pretty liar. Lie to me again. Lie to me for all eternity as long as you're here with me. *Alive.*"

That finger went up again over her lips, trapping her words in. But she didn't have any to say as they were lodged in her throat, her head, her heart.

"Tell me the truth so I can fuck you however you want. I can't go along with this charade anymore, and before I worship all of you, you need to know that I already knew. Until the day I die, I will never stop fucking loving *you*." Tears welled in his eyes after he said the last word, his voice a whisper.

Her hands shook, the sentence finally forming as she moved to get off of him and stood. She could tell he wanted to hold her down, but instead, he got up directly across from her.

"You know I'm Tip." Her voice came out shaky.

He nodded. "It was the letter in your satchel that made me certain, but there were other things. It was the way you tugged your ear, knowing where things were, the look on your face when you found me with the prostitute. Did you really think I wouldn't put it together? You could be in dragon form, unable to speak, and I would still recognize you soon enough. I know you better than anyone."

"I know," she said softly. And if Jack had been in her position, she would have detected who he really was, too.

"Then why didn't you tell me? Why make up such an elaborate story?" His voice grew louder, angrier. "We never lied to each other!"

"Because you were fucking someone who wasn't me!" She rushed forward and cupped a hand over his mouth. "And I'm glad you did because I realized how selfish it would be if you knew the whole truth anyway. You deserve to be free, Jack. *Free.* So I'm going to give that to you now. Jackseith Arel Diosyll, forget that I'm Tip. I release you, Jackseith Arel Diosyll."

Ozma slowly dropped her hand, watching Jack's gaze focus on her. Tears of her own pricked at her eyes at what she'd done.

A cold smirk crossed Jack's face. "Sorry, Blossom. True names don't work like that."

Chapter Sixteen

Jack

Jack's anger exploded through his chest. Ozma tried to use his *true name* to make him forget! As if he wouldn't realize the truth all over again. As if he didn't have a right to know. If she wanted him to be free, she never should've come back to the farm. She should've continued to let Jack think the Tip he knew was dead.

"Please forget it," she practically begged.

"How dare you?" he seethed. "How dare you do this to me? Did you think you could just sweep back into my life, lie through your teeth, and leave? No harm done?"

"I had to come back to kill Mombi and the Wizard."

Jack winced. She came back from the dark place and, instead of seeking him out, returned only for revenge. "You never loved me at all, did you?"

"Of course, I did," she said with tears in her eyes. "I *do*. But you deserve to be free."

A growl slipped through Jack's teeth and he stepped closer, grasping Ozma's shoulder. "Don't tell me what I deserve. My choices have *never* been my own—none except to love you. And now you want to take that decision from me too?"

Ozma's hands closed around his forearm, tugging until his grip loosened. "That's not what I'm doing."

"It's exactly what you're doing." His heart thumped painfully and he stumbled back a step. "But I can never be free of you, Blossom. No matter how much you push me away or lie, my heart is yours."

When he thought Tip was dead, he'd wanted to live to honor him. Not with his actions, because sleeping his way through Loland was a desperate attempt to numb his own pain, but to *remember*. Everyone died twice—once when they passed away and again when no one remembered they'd ever existed. Jack had wanted to keep Tip alive in that way... But if there was no *first* death, then there was no reason to worry about the second.

Jack looked urgently into Ozma's eyes, imploring her to see how much he loved her. It didn't matter what she looked like—Tip was her and she was Tip. But she said nothing as she held his gaze.

"You're killing me," Jack whispered.

"I'm sorry," Ozma said, her chin quivering. "I *never* meant to hurt you."

Jack laughed humorlessly. "You're doing a hell of a job of it anyway."

If they weren't trapped in an underground cave, he would've left then. Hid himself away somewhere and allowed himself to have a good cry before he decided what to do. Though, if he were being honest with himself, he already knew that he would forgive Ozma. After his anger ebbed, he would forgive her lies if she only loved him. *Really* loved him. None of the self-sacrificing bullshit.

But there was nowhere to go to nurse his wounds, so instead, he swept up his wet clothes and pulled them back on—freezing be damned. His churning emotions would keep him warm until he could figure out how to save them both.

Jack paced, his gaze sweeping from one side of the cave to the other in search of a way out. Smooth walls. Sky-high ceiling.

Think, Jack, think. His thoughts refused to drift away from Ozma though. He tried not to notice her near the wall where she had lay down and curled in a ball, shivering, with her dress pulled tight around her shoulders like a blanket. Goosebumps covered his own body and his toes were numb. *Find a way out.*

If he froze to death, an escape route wouldn't matter.

"Shit," he mumbled to himself and stalked back to Ozma. She peeked up at him and his heart thudded heavily. *Those damn eyes.* How many times had he begged the universe to bring his lover back? How many times had he promised to do *anything* for just one more day? Too many times to count. And what was he doing now that his prayers had been answered? His chest caved, taking all his walls with it.

"I'm sorry," he blurted.

A crease formed between Ozma's brows. "For what?"

"Losing my temper."

"It's not like I didn't deserve it," she said between chattering teeth.

Jack removed his clothes once again and knelt beside her so they could warm each other. "Let's not talk about it anymore, okay?" He laid down and inched closer.

"Fine." Ozma immediately wound her arms around his waist and snuggled into his chest. "I have to confess one more thing to you," she mumbled, "and then you'll understand. But I never stopped loving you, Jack. Not once."

One more thing? What else could there be?

"Tell me tomorrow," he said.

Tomorrow he would ask. Now he would allow himself a few hours of happiness. *She still loves me.* He sighed into Ozma's hair and pulled her flush against him. This time, he would make sure nothing happened to her.

The lack of light in the cave made it difficult to tell how long they had been asleep. Jack pried himself away from Ozma's body, his back still cold from the lack of skin-to-skin contact, and stretched. He'd slept on worse, but it didn't make the stone any more comfortable. It was pure luck that his arm hadn't lost circulation.

Ozma curled in on herself at the loss of his shared warmth, covering her breasts in the process. Jack wished he could've seen them again, but hopefully there would be another chance soon. Ozma *loved him* and had seemed willing to show him that. Maybe she would again.

Thoughts of them fucking in the past flashed through Jack's mind. Tip bent over. His smooth back. His soft moans. The taste of him on Jack's tongue and the feel of Tip's lips all over his body, his cock. They had always worked well together. He very much wanted to see her beautiful face flush as he pleasured her and tangled his fingers in her silky golden hair.

Shit.

Now was not the time to get himself overly excited.

Once his back cracked twice, he glared up at the opening they'd fallen through again. They were well and truly fucked. If only the walls weren't so smooth, there would be a chance they could climb out. But the vines were too high up for—

"Ozma!" he shouted despite her nearness.

A small shriek echoed through the cave and a few of the blue bugs went dark. "What happened? Are you okay?"

"Sorry, I didn't mean to frighten you." He scooped up his now-dry clothing and began tugging it on. "Get dressed. We're leaving."

"What?" Ozma patted around for her dress. "How?"

Jack yanked his shirt over his head and grinned, then wiggled his fingers. "Magic."

He couldn't believe he hadn't thought of it the night before. Maybe it was the pain of smacking into the water, or the shock of the cold, or the revelation of Ozma's truth that had kept the magical option from his thoughts.

Jack quickly spun on his heels and held his palms up toward the opening. *Grow,* he urged the vines. They crept down, down, down like snakes, groaning from the quick growth. Twisting and curling, they slowly descended from the top of the cave. When the ends were nearly at the water, Jack stopped them.

Form a net. It would be quicker and safer than climbing.

The vines slid over each other, up and down, making neat rows as if it were a basket they wove. They kept going until the edge of the vines reached their rocky platform.

With a cocky smirk, Jack turned to Ozma and held out his hand. Ozma's mouth dropped open in awe.

"After you, Blossom," he said with a chuckle.

Ozma brushed her fingers against the net and gave the vines a tug. "I've scaled worse. It seems sturdy enough." She shrugged, stepping out onto the vines.

Let's hope so. There was no reason it shouldn't be though, so he simply followed her carefully onto the net. "Going up," he said once they were both steady.

Lift us, he thought at the vines. Their energy pulsed through him like a second heartbeat. The vines creaked under their weight as the net rose, inching closer and closer to the surface. When they were near enough to pull themselves up, Jack reached out mentally to tell them to stop their ascent. The magic tingled through him and the vines eased to a jerky halt.

Ozma went first, climbing free of the cave as if it were nothing more than hopping over a fallen log. She seemed more agile than she'd been as Tip. More free and sure of herself. It was a wonderful change to witness after all he'd seen her go through in the past. He wanted to know more, see what was different about her, learn how she'd grown into the fae she was now.

"Onward," he said with a flourish once they both stood outside the tree. It had looked so inviting the night before, but now he would steer clear of trees with caves.

The farther they walked, the more the sun thawed the last bits of him. Jack's joints no longer felt stiff and his shoulders relaxed as he finally stopped hugging himself. There was only one uncomfortable thing left to deal with.

"So…" Jack hesitated, unsure whether he wanted the answer yet or not. *Better to get it out of the way.* "What's the last thing you have to tell me?"

Ozma twisted her hands together. "Wait until we get on the boat, and I'll explain everything."

Jack clenched his jaw and nodded. What were a few more hours when he probably didn't want to know anyway?

Chapter Seventeen

Ozma

Ozma and Jack trekked through the forest until midday. With each step, the map in her veins pulsed, pointing her toward the sea, her destination. Hours ago, they'd crossed into Hiland, but it seemed no different than Loland, only more dips and even taller trees covered in leaves the size of Ozma's head.

She hadn't spoken to Jack, and he hadn't spoken to her. The silence between them was tangible, and she knew he had questions. But he wasn't the only one—she did too. The night before flashed in her head—his mouth on hers, her body pressed to his, her attempting to use his true name to forget.

How could she have done that? But it would have been for him. Perhaps it was unfair for her to have even tried that, but she loved him enough to let him go.

Now he knew who she was, though. She should have known it couldn't be kept a secret forever. And he'd been right about one thing. If she'd truly wanted him to be free, then why had she come back for him? Why hadn't she realized it would've been better to let him be? Either way, she'd always known she had to free him from Mombi. She'd spent the last two years thinking about her reunion with Jack. A childish dream.

The quiet—his quiet, her quiet—spread and spread around her until it became too much. She opened her mouth to finally speak when he grasped her arm, pulling her to a stop.

"I hear it," Jack said, biting his lip as he stared ahead.

"Hear what?" She drew out her dagger from her hip and lifted it. They were so close to the shore and she didn't want to be slowed down again.

"The ocean." Jack released her arm and took a step forward. "Do you hear it too?"

She tilted her head and perked her ears. When an almost magical sound floated around her, she lowered her dagger. The lapping of water against shore, sea birds cawing, the wind singing. "It's beautiful."

A smile spread across Jack's cheeks, reminding her of how he'd been before she'd gone to the dark place. "Remember when we talked about seeing the sea one day?" he asked.

"One day we'll visit the sea, and I'll worship your body in it until you've come as many times as you wish, not caring who sees us fuck."

Tip felt his cheeks heat. "I hope that's a promise."

"Oh, it's more than that," Jack said, swiping his tongue against the glistening pearl at the head of Tip's cock, then placing his lips around the length.

Ozma swallowed hard, the memory drawing a warmth in her like it did back then. "Did you still plan on coming here?"

"No…" The smile fell from his face. And she knew it was because he hadn't wanted to go alone, without her.

Something about seeing that broken expression made her heart hurt. She was here now, and they would look upon the sea together. Perhaps not worship each other's bodies there, at least not this time.

"Well"—Ozma shoved him playfully—"looks like I'll be seeing it first."

His lips parted and his eyes widened. With a laugh, she took off at a heavy sprint, just as she used to do when they would race to the lake.

"You're such a cheat!" Jack yelled.

She threw her head back and laughed again when a few curses flew from his lips. Clumped branches decorating the ground slowed her pace. As she was about to regain her lead, Jack's strong arms gripped her waist, lifting and whirling her around. After setting her down, he took off, chuckling.

"You!" she screamed, skirting around trees and ducking under branches, until she finally caught up with him.

Ozma yanked him to her by the back of his tunic, and they both stopped when voices echoed ahead.

"The port," she said, heading in the direction of the sounds, shoving aside shrubbery blooming with fragrant red and black berries.

The world before her opened to a silver sea, reflecting the sun's rays, and a gasp escaped her mouth. It was nothing like she'd imagined and more amazing than she could have believed. Ships and rafts of all colors lined the sparkling water, the soft swells bobbing them in a rhythmic motion. Glittery golds, sparkling blues, shimmery pinks. All with bright white sails flapping in the wind. Numerous fae carrying crates or barrels loaded up their ships for travel. Other fae delivered their supplies by foot, stag, or wagon.

"We have to find out which ship is heading for Orkland and sneak on board." She surveyed the area, reading the names on the sides of several green ships flecked with yellow.

"Not a raft." Jack squinted and pointed straight ahead. "I think that's our prize."

Ozma focused on a dark charcoal ship and studied the side where letters were painted in a deep red, forming the words, *The Wizard.*

She rolled her eyes at the name, but she was almost sure it would be destined for Orkland.

"Let's blend in, shall we?" she said, straightening.

He nodded and motioned her forward. "Follow me. I have

an idea."

As she remained alongside Jack, crossing the soft lavender-colored sand, several fae with horns sprouting from their heads carried baskets of jewels past them.

"Excuse me," Jack called to a female draped in pink silk, her horns wrapped in matching ribbon. "Which ship is headed for Orkland?"

"Right there." She pointed at the charcoal ship. "Perhaps you would care to join us on our boat instead? For a cost, I can take you to the Isle of Phreex where there will be endless pleasure." Her tone came out silky as her gaze roamed over Jack in a flirtatious manner. Jealousy stormed through Ozma's veins, and she drew her hands into tight fists.

Jack made a tsking sound. "Not today."

"Your loss." The female shrugged and sauntered, her hips swaying seductively, toward a golden boat.

"You weren't tempted?" Ozma asked, turning to face Jack, fighting the clench of her teeth.

"Mmm. Having my spine ripped through my throat sounds really pleasurable to me." He grinned. "How about you?"

Ozma's eyes widened when she recalled the tale so long ago about the Isle of Phreex. The female fae who lived there would bring males back to tumble, which hypnotized their prey, causing the males to crave more and more pleasure, until they slowly went mad, chopping off pieces of their own selves to feed to the females.

"Let's go," she said and barely missed stumbling into a group of brownies headed toward *The Wizard.*

Jack and Ozma stood at the pier and watched as fae carried empty glass vials in buckets onto the ship. Ozma followed them onto the deck, and Jack yanked her down behind a stack of wooden boxes, just as a tall male elf with red eyes, a shirt to match, and golden studs along his pointed ears, rounded a corner. The fae was tall and broad with golden skin and hair the darkest of blacks.

"This was all we could bring, Tik-Tok," a brownie missing two fingers said.

He ripped the vials from the brownies' hands before shooing them off the ship and slipping somewhere out of view.

"Now what?" Ozma asked.

"Below deck?" His answer sounded more like a question.

She cocked a brow, eyeing the obsidian door and its sapphire handle. "And what if someone's there? Or what if it's locked?"

"We'll figure it out soon enough, won't we, Blossom?"

Ozma puckered her lips, wondering if it would be better to just remain right where they were.

"Ah, I missed that look too," he purred, tugging her toward the door.

She kept her feet feather-light beside him. Holding her breath, she drew open the door. A set of wooden stairs lay before her and a flowery scent hit her nose. No shuffling sounds came from below, so she quietly walked down the steps. Jack trailed closely at her heels after he closed the door behind them.

At the last step, Ozma breathed again while Jack searched the large space. The walls were lined with wooden barrels and crates of wine bottles cluttered the area. There were several open rooms without doors that held more crates, stacked high—these filled with faerie fruit and vials containing different colored liquids. Some sort of potions?

A scuffing of footsteps sounded from the other side of the door at the top of the stairs.

"Fuck," Jack whispered, pointing her to one of the rooms as the door creaked open.

Ozma slipped inside and darted beside Jack into a corner behind the crates. She peered out a narrow crack between the crates as two fae entered the room. The male from before—Tik-Tok—and another female with short red hair. They each set down sacks of something.

"The Wizard keeps demanding more fruit, but don't they have enough over there?" the female asked. Silver hoops pierced the entire edges of both her pointed ears.

"You would think. But the fiends' cravings keep getting stronger." Tik-Tok raked a gloved hand through his sleek black hair.

"I don't see how fruit does anything to the fae," the female said. "It should only affect the humans."

"It just does. Quit asking questions unless you want to end up like them when Mombi returns for our next shipment." He shrugged. "And don't forget to lock the door this time. We don't need the fucking wine disappearing again."

Their feet pounded up the steps as they exited, followed by the echo of the lock turning.

Ozma relaxed against the wall of the ship. They would be trapped down here for a while, but they'd made it.

"Cozy place we have here for the night, isn't it?" Jack leaned back beside her, stretching out his legs as much as he could.

"Is that sarcasm?"

"No." His warm breath brushed her ear, and she held back a shiver at his nearness. "Now that we're here … what did you plan on telling me? There's nothing you could say that would make me leave your side. I'm the freest when I'm with you."

The boat eased forward, the hull rocking side to side. Ozma's nerves were on edge, but not because this was her first time on a ship. She had no idea how Jack would react to what she was about to say. She bit the inside of her cheek as she spoke, "I'm the queen."

"That you are." He tapped the end of her nose. "We can play all the games you want later, Blossom. But for now, tell me."

She needed to be straightforward and tell him the entire truth—he deserved to know. Should have known earlier, but she couldn't change the past several days. "Lurline, my mother, was a faerie, which is why I had wings before Mombi burned them. My father was King Pastoria, and because they're both dead, that makes me queen."

Jack's brow furrowed. "Queen of *what*?"

"Oz…"

He blinked several times, his mouth parting. "Oz," he finally repeated.

"Yes. All of Oz."

When he didn't say anything else and remained still as a statue, she continued, "You've always wanted to be free, Jack. And I came to the conclusion recently that this would only be trapping you again. I wouldn't be able to travel the world anytime I wanted. Like we'd talked about…"

"Is being queen something you want, though?"

Ozma had thought about it over and over, and had even contemplated giving the throne to Reva. But something in her couldn't, as though she were created for this purpose—to make Oz good again and keep it that way. "Yes, it's something I want."

"I'm not worthy of you, Blossom. It took me forever to believe I was before, but now you're a queen. *The queen.*" His shoulders remained tight, his throat bobbing.

"Jack, you're not Mombi's slave anymore. She made you feel this way—she made you believe you were nothing." *Made me believe I was nothing too.*

"I've already proved what a bastard I am." Jack's head drooped. "While you were banished by Mombi, what was I doing? I fucked and I fucked and I *fucked.* I'm such a piece of shit. But you, you can do anything you want. I always knew that."

Her chest sank at his words because he truly believed this of himself. "You're not nothing—you're everything, and a king to me. You always have been. Even that damn pumpkin patch felt like a kingdom at times because you were by my side. But now we have choices. You can get to know the world … other fae." As much as it ached to say it, he deserved to make his own decisions.

"That's the thing." He held her gaze. "I've been around other fae and know that there's no one I'd rather have than you. Yet you haven't—you've only known me. Perhaps it's me who should free you to discover if there's someone better suited." He clenched his jaw, as though those last words had to be forced from his perfect lips.

"Damn it, Jack," she whisper-shouted. "You know I choose you. Every time." She threw her arms around him, holding him tight.

He lifted her into his lap and rested his chin on her head, his fingers interlacing with her hair. "Then we have that matter solved."

For a long while, they stayed in that position, and even though the room remained silent, it was as if their bodies were speaking to each other, comforting, apologizing.

Finally, Ozma peered up at him, the angles of his face, his hazel irises. Those eyes that could sweep her anywhere.

Jack's gaze fell to her and he smiled. "So, since you're my queen, what are you going to order me to do first?"

Ozma shook her head, about to give him a sarcastic reply, when his lips crashed to hers, taking her by surprise. She inhaled, savoring the flavor of his lips as she kissed him back with equal hunger, her tongue tasting every inch of his mouth.

"I don't think there will be much time for kissing once we get to Orkland," he rasped.

"Keep kissing me then." *And don't ever stop.*

Jack's strong body shifted as he lay her on the floor, hovering above her. A naughty grin formed on his face as he leaned forward and whispered in her ear, "I don't want to kiss *only* your lips. I want to kiss here." His tongue flicked the side of her neck. "Here." He moved down her body, kissing her through her clothing, above her breast. "Certainly here." Then he traveled to her navel, pressing his lips gently there. "And, finally, here." His fingers skimmed up her dress, against her uncovered thigh, so very close to the place that desperately wanted to feel his caress.

"Remove my dress then." She didn't care how he got it off as long as it was gone—now.

In answer, he drew up her dress, agonizingly slow. She pulled it from her body and lay completely bare before him. He'd seen her several times like this, but somehow it felt different.

Ozma placed her hand against his heart, feeling the thudding pulse against her palm. "Do you really like me in my true form?"

Jack tugged his tunic up and over his head, then rested his chest against hers, their hearts beating in sync. His warm skin ignited hers like a flame held to a candle. "How could I not?" His hands shook as he held her. Jack had never been nervous about anything.

"Why are you trembling?" she asked, wondering if she'd done something wrong.

"I lost the house you built for me," he whispered, his voice cracking. "That was the important thing in my satchel."

Ozma's hands trembled then too, because he had always loved her as much as she loved him. "It doesn't matter. A house is what you make of it." No longer was she worried about what he would think about her body, or if he would compare it to her old one. She knew he would love it regardless.

She reached between them, unlaced the tie of his pants, and shoved them down. Jack kicked them off the remainder of the way until there were only their bodies sinking into one another.

Jack slowly kissed the place at her neck, grazing it with his teeth, and sending a shiver through her from head to toe. He again drifted to her breast, her navel, until his lips connected with the tender spot on her inner thigh. Her hands entwined with his soft hair, wanting him to come closer, to taste her.

As his hot tongue stroked her center, an intense feeling swarmed through her that she hadn't expected. It was much different than having a cock—more intimate, as his tongue pressed inside her, swirling, licking. Her nerves lit up, creating their own blue starlight. She tried not to moan too loud as his lips moved between her folds. Ozma's hands tightened in his hair as his rhythm picked up—she didn't want him to stop. Not now. Not ever. But she wanted something else—*harder*—to fill her.

"Jack." She lifted his head from between her thighs, his lips shiny from devouring her. "Give me everything."

His gaze dilated with understanding. "Are you sure? We don't have to yet."

That was true. They were on a ship, behind stacks of crates, with guards above them. But she was used to sneaking around with Jack and them pleasuring each other in secret places, hoping not to be discovered. "It's been two years. I'm plenty ready."

"As you wish." Jack grinned mischievously, his wicked tongue traveling up her stomach as he planted kisses. His lips closed around her nipple, sucking and licking. Her body tightened with need as he moved to the other one, repeating the motions before coming to her mouth.

She gently bit his bottom lip, making him groan as his lower body drew closer. The tip of his cock skimmed her entrance, and her center throbbed at the caress. A nervousness poured over her as it had when she'd done this the first time with him as a male. But yearning overpowered that. His hardened length pushed into her, the pressure causing her to gasp, her back arching.

"Are you all right?" he asked, his thumb brushing her cheek.

Ozma nodded and Jack pressed farther in, little by little, stretching her until the pain relinquished. Her gaze held his as he slowly moved. Then, when she needed more, she gripped his ass, urging him on.

Jack smirked. "I knew you would get tired of this pace." He rolled his hips forward, shaking them both, filling her with pleasure. He thrust again and again, her legs wrapping around his waist as he drummed into her, until she needed even more.

She rolled them over to his back, her legs now cradling his hips. They stared at each other, his hand cupping her breast, his thumb drawing subtle lines over her nipple.

Holding back the desire to grind her hips forward, she leaned closer, kissing him ever so gently on the lips. "I love you," Ozma murmured, her breath striking his mouth.

Before he had time to return the sentiment, Ozma rolled against him, his cock rubbing her center in a delicious manner.

This position was new for her, and she wasn't sure if she was doing it right. As if knowing what she needed, Jack gripped her waist, helping her ride him with steady back and forth motions. When she became more attuned to it, confident, she arched her back, rolling her hips in slow circles, over and over.

Their pace kicked up, faster and faster until a strong heightening sensation, enveloped her, consumed her. She had to control herself from screaming Jack's name as a blissful wave of pleasure stormed over her. Ozma's body shook as miniature earthquakes rocketed from her center to her toes, her fingertips, *everywhere*. But she didn't stop, not until Jack also felt the beautiful euphoria.

A moment later, Jack groaned, seeming to hold back his shout too as his cock jerked inside her. Before pulling out of her, he sat up, holding her against his chest, both breathing hard.

"I love you too." He pressed his lips to hers in a delicate kiss and smirked. "My queen."

Rolling her eyes, she rested her forehead on his. "My king."

CHAPTER EIGHTEEN

JACK

The ship gently rocked beneath Jack and Ozma. They'd both dressed quickly after they'd finished fucking in case anyone came back downstairs, but Jack wished circumstances were different. He wanted to learn every curve of her body with delicate touches. To brush his fingertips over her bare back, her shoulders, her arms, her breasts. To skim his lips and tongue over her collarbones and up the side of her neck. He wanted to feel her heartbeat beneath his hand as she calmed after they fucked.

A queen.

He winced. Was he really up to the task of ruling the land of Oz at her side? On one hand, it felt almost like protection. A shield for the future if they were lucky enough to win. After everything Mombi had put them through, he desperately wanted that. But… Ozma was a queen. A literal queen. With subjects to rule and laws to make and everything else that came with that.

Fuck.

There would probably be assassins lining up to kill her. And him too if she truly made him her king. *Oh shit.* He was *not* ready for that kind of responsibility. What did he know about the world? He'd been confined to the farm and the market. At least Ozma had learned how to survive in the dark place and about the world from Reva. A king had to manage foreign affairs and … and … other things Jack had no idea about. Because they hadn't been in their hidden adventure book and he was a fucking clueless farmhand. A *slave.*

Jack's stomach heaved. They could be caught at any moment and, though he hadn't noticed until minutes after dressing, the ship's movements weren't settling well with him. The musty scent of the ship and the salty tang of the ocean swirled through him like poison. He could *not* be ill here. The loud retching would undoubtedly bring attention below deck, as there were fae directly above them. A light shower of dust rained down with every metallic *thunk* of someone's footsteps.

"Are you well?" Ozma asked, brushing the hair from Jack's eyes.

He licked his lips. "Nauseous."

"You're sick?" Her palm pressed against his forehead. "Did you eat something strange before we left? Or did you use too much magic getting us out of the cave?"

"I don't—" He paused to swallow the excess saliva flooding his mouth. *Fucking hell.* Jack shook his head, which only made everything worse. He lay back and closed his eyes. "How much longer?" he asked, fully aware there were hours ahead.

"It feels like less than a day by boat," she said. "Do you need anything? Some fruit?"

"Shh," he managed, but that was all he could force himself to say. If anything else left his mouth, it wouldn't be words.

Ozma settled beside him and ran her fingers through his hair. "Perhaps it's just the motion of the ship. Once, in the dark place, Reva and I thought to cross a lake using a giant lily pad. Turned out that they were attached to creatures beneath the murky surface. I think it felt us climb aboard because it started swimming in circles so fast that all we could do was hold on. We didn't stop for nearly two days. I was sure we were done for."

"What was it?" he whispered. Being trapped in this ship with danger above them was bad enough—he couldn't imagine what she'd felt then.

"What was what?"

Jack cracked his eyes to look at Ozma. "The fae beneath the water. What was it?"

"I'm not sure the beings there were fae, but we never saw what it was. As soon as we passed close enough to shore, we jumped off and ran in case it was able to follow." She smiled gently down at him. "Now, let me distract you with details of what our home will look like once the Wizard is dead."

"Like a palace," he said with a smirk.

"Hush," Ozma said, playfully smacking his shoulder. "We might have to live there sometimes, but it won't be our home. We'll have a secret place away from the city with a short stone fence around the yard. There won't be a gate, though—nothing to close us in. I'm going to fill it with flowers of every color and, outside the fence, we'll plant vegetables and fruit orchards, but *not* pumpkins. Any fae will be allowed to take what they need. We'll plant everything far enough away so we have privacy. Inside, we'll have a large bedroom and a library full of adventure books."

Jack's smile widened. *A life.* As they'd planned—only now, it was truly possible. "Just like the book we had before?"

"Like that," she agreed. "But different ones too. All kinds of adventures."

Jack closed his eyes and focused on Ozma's gentle voice as she described in precise detail what else they would have. All of it sounded perfect … assuming they survived long enough for it to become a reality.

"Jack," Ozma whispered. "Jack, wake up."

He cracked his eyes open—when had he fallen asleep? "Hmm?"

"I think we're here." She stood and tilted her head to the ceiling. "They're shouting."

Jack forced himself to get up, his stomach a bit calmer than before, and listened. A deep voice called out to drop anchor and tie down the sails. Then a loud *splash* hit the water on the other side of the hull. Feet pounded back and forth and wood scraped against wood. More shouts rang up, a mixture of voices, giving directions he couldn't quite make out.

"How do you want to get out of here?" Ozma asked. "Once they unlock the door, they'll probably start unloading all of this."

And catch us. "Guess we'll have to play it by ear." There was little else they could do besides hide and try to get out of there unseen. If they had anything of value, perhaps they could've bribed a brownie or two to look the other way. Sadly, all they had was Ozma's title and that meant nothing until she retook the Land of Oz.

Ozma yanked on his arm, pulling him behind a barrel with her. She quickly put a finger to his lips to stop his protest. "Shh. Someone's coming."

Jack's heart thumped wildly in his chest as he crouched behind the fruit. Two sets of footsteps hit the stairs in tandem, one heavier than the other. "Grab the food first," Tik-Tok ordered. "Make sure the fiends are fed so we can make it to the shelter without killing any of them."

"Yes, sir," a squeaky brownie replied.

"Get started and I'll send the others down."

Tik-Tok's heavier feet thumped upstairs again and Jack peeked around the barrel. The brownie shifted one of the crates from the top of a pile. It tilted precariously and her small, withered hands struggled to balance it again.

An idea sparked in Jack's mind as the first apple tumbled down on the brownie's head. She let out a small yelp of fear and Jack gave Ozma's hand a squeeze. "She's going to drop that," he whispered, "and we're going to use it as a distraction to get out of here."

"What? No!" Ozma replied. "The commotion will only bring more of them down here."

And the more fae that came, the better their movements would blend in with theirs. Jack nodded once. "Exactly."

The crate finally toppled on the brownie, apples rolling everywhere, and Jack prepared to run. "Stay with me," he said and crept toward the stairs.

"What was that?" someone called from above. "Everything all right down there?"

Jack tucked Ozma beneath the stairs and squeezed in beside her, just as a handful of brownies and elves hurried into the storage rooms.

"Shit," Tik-Tok shouted. "What *the fuck* did you do now?"

The crushed brownie stumbled over her words as the others quickly gathered the apples.

Now, Jack mouthed. His hands shook slightly with nerves, but this was their chance. He sprang out from behind their hiding spot with Ozma right behind him. Keeping one eye on the brownies, Jack took the stairs two at a time. The distraction worked as well as he'd hoped—the crew's attention was focused wholly on the mess, and his and Ozma's movements were lost in the frenzy to pick up the fruit.

But that was where the success of Jack's plan ended.

More pirates worked the rigging, lugged ropes, and lowered small row boats from the side of *The Wizard*. And every eye swiveled to Jack and Ozma—the pair of fae bolting from the bowels of the ship as if their lives depended on it.

Because they did.

"Jump," Jack yelled as he reached the side of the deck. And he leapt, trusting Ozma would follow. The waves sucked him under just as another body sank down beside him. The warm, salty water stung his eyes, but he kept them open, waiting to see if it was Ozma or someone else. Once the bubbles cleared, he found his beloved reaching out for him.

Jack grabbed Ozma's hand, his lungs begging for air as they surfaced. He glanced at the shore—the distance seemed manageable, but he didn't want to be wrong. "Wait," he rasped. Turning back toward the ship, he fixed his gaze on one of the lowered row boats that was within reach. Jack tilted the side of the boat toward them. "Get in, *quick*."

Ozma heaved herself up over the side and helped Jack in beside her as dozens of fae looked down at them, shouting. Tik-Tok loomed above the rest with an expression of pure fury.

"Leave them," he yelled. His lips curled into a cruel smirk, his red irises blazing. "They have nowhere to go."

Nowhere to go? *The Wizard* was anchored farther out since there wasn't a pier, hence the row boats, but there was most definitely a landmass.

"That's not good," Ozma breathed as Jack was about to row.

"What's—" Jack's gaze landed on the shore. Aquamarine sand sparkled in the fading sunlight and, beyond that, black skeletal trees loomed like shadows. But that wasn't what Ozma was talking about.

On the sand walked dozens of fae. Fae and—Jack squinted—humans. They wore dirty, torn clothing, their hair unkempt. It was the blank expressions paired with ravenous eyes that set Jack's pulse racing though.

"Shit."

"What are they?" Ozma asked.

Damned if I know. Jack swallowed hard. "A huge fucking problem, that's what."

Chapter Nineteen

Ozma

Hisses and growls drifted over the silver sea. Ozma couldn't take her gaze away from the fae and humans hovering at the edge of the forest and on the shore. She hadn't been around many others until recently, but she knew they were not supposed to look like this. The faes' skin had a purplish hue, their pointed ears drooped over, their cheeks sunken. Everything about them appeared hollow, a shadow of what they once were.

As for the humans, their gazes seemed unfocused, their bodies leaning to one side, as though they might topple over at any moment. From what Tik-Tok had said aboard the ship, they were all addicted to faerie fruit on the island. The sprite had told her that there was an enchantment over everyone here, and this wasn't what Ozma had been expecting at all. Perhaps she'd imagined them with pupils dilated a little more, like how Mombi's would get when she ate certain mushrooms. This was so much worse.

Ozma swallowed, her eyes roaming from the fae and humans, to the skeletal black trees with their glistening white leaves and long ivory vines, and back to the crazed faces of the victims, their lingering movements. She chanced a glance over her shoulder toward the ship, its sails down, unmoving.

Tik-Tok still stood there, his arms draped off the side of the ship, his red eyes lazily watching them. A wicked grin spread across his face, replacing his earlier anger.

"Go on. I won't stop you," he called, daring her, then swiping a lock of obsidian hair behind his gold-studded ear. His face was beautiful in a vicious way, and she wondered about his part in all this.

"Ignore him," Jack said.

She focused back on Jack, his hands on the oars, the boat bobbing against the silver water.

Closing her eyes for a moment, she thought of the dark place, the beasts she and Reva had escaped from. Although there had never been as many creatures as this, the beasts there were much faster, their movements unpredictable.

A splash came from near the shore, drawing her gaze straight ahead to two female humans with matted hair hobbling into the water. Ozma placed her hand on the dagger at her hip, but the humans didn't swim. They continued to walk forward, hissing, until their bodies, inch by inch, were taken by the water.

She waited for them to rise to the surface. But they didn't. Not until moments later when their unmoving bodies floated to the top of the swells.

"I wasn't expecting that," Jack said, one orange brow lifted.

Ozma's heart thudded rapidly. They couldn't continue sitting in this boat with Tik-Tok gloating down at them. And if they lingered near the ship too long, would he hunt them down himself?

The vines on the island gave her an idea. She clasped her hand around Jack's arm. "Can you use your magic from here?" He'd been able to do it in the cave, but the vines there had been much closer than these.

Jack thrust a hand forward and twisted it to the side, his teeth clenching. His fingers tightened and loosened, then he shook his head. "No. We're not close enough for me to feel the life in them."

The swarm of corrupted humans and fae opened their mouths wide, hissing, baring their teeth. Their skin was peeling away in areas, revealing inky black muscles. *Rotting.* They were alive but decaying. Another idea came to Ozma, one that would hopefully work. Besides, it was her turn to save Jack.

Standing from the wooden seat, she faced Jack. "I want you to row to shore. Let me distract them."

"Oh no, you don't." Jack reached for her, but it was too late.

She jumped into the warm water, then kicked her legs and pumped her arms, swimming beneath the waves. The sea seemed to caress her flesh, as though it were trying to lure her into staying below the surface.

Silently, she said Jack's name over and over inside her head to not give in to the temptation to turn back. Cutting through the liquid with long motions, Ozma stayed underwater. She would do it for as long as she could before needing air. This was as familiar to her as walking or sleeping. She'd done it at the lake by the pumpkin patch and beneath the eerie waters of the dark place.

Below her, purple and blue striped eels laced through one another. But she couldn't see anything much farther than that—the water wasn't clear enough because of the silver tint and the glittery sheen.

A slow burn started to develop in her lungs. She would need air soon, but she held on a little longer, stroking harder, faster, before finally rising to the surface. As her head broke through the swells, she gulped in as much air as she could. Her gaze darted to the shore, so very near.

The fae hadn't seen her—all their focus was on Jack, who was rowing and glaring at her at the same time. She smiled and shrugged, because he would see her purpose soon enough.

Ozma cut across the water, until she could touch the ground, then ran the rest of the way, her bare feet finally striking dry sand.

Her body was soaking wet, her dress heavy, as she drew the blade from her hip. "Over here!" she shouted.

All eyes turned to her in sync. Ozma bounced on the sand, waving her hands in the air. "That's right! Come on!" As soon as the swarm started toward her, she jolted for the trees. Two fae, with black gore dripping from their lips, pushed out from the forest before she could get to her destination. As they growled, their bodies swaying, Ozma lifted her dagger and drove it through the male's chest, then the female's heart. Dark red blood oozed from the wounds as the two fae slumped to the ground with a thump.

A human crawling near Ozma's leg snapped her blackened teeth, and she drew a blade across the female's throat. There'd be no saving any of these humans. Whatever Mombi did to them was too dark to bring them back. Unintelligible noises escaped the human's lips as Ozma lunged for a tree, striking it with her foot to give her leverage. Her arms easily caught the branch above, just as another fae swiped at her legs and missed.

Swinging herself up, Ozma folded her legs around the branch and quickly scanned the area for Jack. The boat stood empty at the edge of the water, but then she spotted him farther away, moving toward her with both his hands raised, shaking, like using his magic was too much.

The swarm must have heard his footsteps because they stopped batting their hands at the air below her branch. Slowly, they turned to face him, hissing, their jaws unclamping.

Ozma was about to leap from the tree, when a white thorn-covered vine shot forward, piercing a fae through the eye, spraying blood. It drove out the back of his head and struck two more behind him. Then two more behind them. More vines came, snaking and curving around the remaining fae and humans. The vines snapped and cracked, and with one fluid motion, they pulled tight, cutting all the bodies in two through their middles.

Jack continued to slash his shaking hands in the air, making the vines whip, then slicing the heads clean off another group. Blood splashed across the sand until all that was left were torn bodies.

In the distance, growling reverberated within the trees. *More…* And they would be heading this way. This time it sounded like too many.

"I think we need to go." Jack ran toward her, his curls damp with sweat. "My magic is still too new, and I don't know how much longer it will last."

"Let's hurry." Grabbing a twisted branch above her, she swung across it to another and another, then let her feet hit the ground a bit farther into the forest. She wiped the blood on her arm, from her kills, against her dress.

Jack was already beside her, brow arched. "I like how you move."

She grasped him by the tunic and yanked him forward.

As they hurried past trees, stepping over fields of black mushrooms with lavender spots, she still wondered if Tik-Tok and the others from the ship would come after them.

"I hope we find the Wizard soon, so we can get off this fucking island," Jack said, hopping over a log.

"Shouldn't be too long." But she wasn't sure. By the map in her veins, she could tell the island wasn't large, yet she didn't know if Oz would be close by or at the opposite end somewhere.

Above them, shriveled, blackened fruit dangled. Mombi's doing. They all oozed dark liquid that matched what coated the swarm's mouths.

Jack wrinkled his nose. "Whatever you do, eat nothing here."

Ozma rolled her eyes when a crunching sound came from ahead, along with something like gurgling and a horrid odor.

"Jack, stop!" she whisper-shouted, latching on to his sleeve. "And don't use your magic." It would be too easy for them to be detected if the Wizard was staying somewhere close by. Hopefully, their incident at the front of the island wouldn't get back to Oz too soon.

They both stopped, listened, then slowly walked the mushroom path. Keeping her feet light, Ozma took a few more steps toward an opening in the trees. Her eyes widened at what she saw through the slits in the leaves.

Dead bodies of fae, rotting and festering, were sprawled across the forest. Their stench permeated the air, and Ozma covered her mouth so she wouldn't lose her stomach. However, there weren't only dead fae, but live ones too, feasting and sucking on the blackened bodies.

Chapter Twenty

Jack

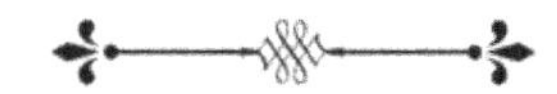

What. The. Actual. Fuck.

Fae and human addicts attacking them was one thing—Jack and Ozma were live prey—but *this*? Jack's gaze latched onto a particularly ghastly human with more exposed muscle than skin, and a black hole where his nose should've been. The human snapped a dead fae's finger off, tendons stretching as the digit was pulled free, and stuck the rough end into his mouth.

And sucked.

Bile burned its way up Jack's throat. This was too much. Far, far too much. The gods-forsaken pumpkin farm seemed like fucking paradise to him now. Even being enslaved to Mombi was better than any of this, though he knew the witch was responsible for these creatures. She must've used her black magic on the fruit which created monsters, likely to quash any threats to the Wizard that reached the island. But, on the farm, there were no monsters—only a nasty old crone who was too fond of swinging her cane. Usually at him. Not to mention, the farm didn't smell like the inside of a dead swine's asshole.

"We should go before they notice us," Ozma whispered in

Jack's ear.

"Right." Jack forced back a cough and nodded to his left. It was the direction they had been heading when they'd paused. Going toward the monsters was clearly out of the question, as was going back toward the beach. They could only hope the only way left was the *right* way.

Ozma followed him as they crept around the field. He kept his eyes and ears trained on the rotting horde, expecting them to attack at any moment. So, when Ozma lunged and knocked him to the ground, he was completely caught off guard.

A growl vibrated above him, sending fear straight down to his marrow. Ozma let out a strangled scream. Her legs thrashed where she lay across Jack's back. He tried to shove himself free, but the weight of her and the addict was too much. He was pinned. Suddenly, he felt Ozma rip her dagger from her waist.

Jack clawed at the ground and managed to drag himself a few inches out from beneath the fight. Then everything was silent. The weight baring down on him doubled. Jack struggled to pull the rancid air into his lungs. *What the fuck is going on?*

"Get"—Ozma growled and shifted her weight—"off."

A body rolled down beside Jack's head. One Ozma had clearly just slaughtered, and the sight left him light-headed. He could've lived the rest of his life without seeing a toothless kobold, blue eyes milky and skin molting, with a dagger jutting from his forehead.

"Fuck," Jack spat, rolling to face Ozma. "Are you all right?"

Ozma stood over the dead kobold with blood sprayed over her face and neck. Her breaths came in great heaves as she nodded and retrieved her dagger. In the distance, predatory snarls carried through the air. "Are you?"

"Yes." He rose from the ground and wiped the blood from her cheeks. She'd saved his life. Drove a blade straight through the fae's skull. If it didn't appear to be half decomposed, he would've said it were impossible, but the bone seemed to crumble around the weapon. "I need to keep what's left of my magic for Oz or I'd cage the field off."

"Yes," she agreed as the growls deepened into something more feral. "But we can't stay here."

They needed to move, and fast. Jack and Ozma sprinted away as quietly as possible. Every so often, one of them would step on a stick that had fallen from a skeletal tree and the crack rumbled like thunder in his ears. There were a few leaves on the ground that crunched below their feet, sounding as if someone was ringing a dinner bell. *Here we are. Come and get us.* A shudder ran through Jack's body.

After what felt like ages, they stopped near a shallow stream and guzzled the cool water. Black fruit hung within an arm's length of the bank but none of what dripped from the rotten skin reached the clear water. Oz would need to keep the fresh water supply disinfected for his own purposes. The fading sunlight shone off the surface, showcasing the smooth pebbles at the bottom and the tiny red and yellow turtles that hurried far from Jack and Ozma's cupped hands. *Cute little buggers,* Jack thought. Probably the only cute fucking things here.

"Look," Ozma called. "There."

Jack followed her gaze and caught a glimpse of green light glowing through the trees on the other side of the stream. *The Wizard of Oz.* Jack had only spoken to Oz briefly the times he'd come to the farm, but leave it to that smug son of a bitch to hide on an island while using obvious magic to give away his location. Ozma led the way closer and paused at the edge of the clearing.

A green, domed barrier glimmered faintly over a small stone house, smoke billowing from the chimney, with six smaller sheds spaced out along the outer edges. Each smaller building was painted black with different symbols carved into the walls. The grass was worn away where someone had walked back and forth between them and the house, while the rest of the lawn grew too tall. Flowers poured down the sides of boxes beneath the windows, rose bushes needed pruning, and weeds covered a small vegetable garden. Two chickens pecked aimlessly at the ground near the other side of the barrier. Jack wondered if they were there for the eggs or to sacrifice to whatever strange gods the Wizard worshipped.

"Don't touch the barrier," Ozma warned him. "It might alert him to our presence."

"Hadn't planned on it, Blossom." With his luck, it would melt his hand off or send his entire body into shock. That would've created quite the scene but done little else. They needed to get inside somehow—break the barrier or figure out how to get through it unnoticed. Or perhaps it would be easiest to lure the Wizard out... But this was Ozma's plot, so he would let her decide. "What now?"

Ozma chewed on her bottom lip. "It's getting late. Let's make camp and try to think of something helpful."

Jack felt a pang of regret at burning all of the witch's books, despite how dark their magic was. He knew they couldn't cart them all across the Land of Oz, but he just *knew* the answer to this problem would've been in one. There wasn't enough luck in the world for the barrier spell to be on one of the few papers Ozma had saved.

Resigned, Jack nodded. They hadn't heard any feral addicts in a while now, and maybe a bit of sleep would restore some of his power. The magic in his veins still felt weak and what was left ached in the same way his back hurt after a day of pulling weeds. "Let's just be sure to keep an eye out for—"

Cold iron pressed against Jack's neck. It bit into his skin and a line of warm blood trailed down toward his collarbone. Ozma froze where she stood a few steps ahead of him. Her eyes were wide and wild, her jaw hanging open with a mixture of shock and fear that echoed Jack's feelings.

"Hello, little stowaways," a deep voice purred in Jack's ear. The same voice from the ship. The elf with red eyes, jet black hair, and a cruel smirk—Tik-Tok. "I must say, I'm impressed."

Chapter Twenty-One

Ozma

Ozma's heart was stuck in her throat as Tik-Tok held his blade to Jack's neck. She'd seen Jack in predicaments with Mombi, but never as bad as this. But he had magic now. And she desperately wished she did too. She pleaded with wide eyes for Jack to use it, to take a vine and rip Tik-Tok's head clean off. But then she focused on the blade cutting into Jack's flesh, drawing a thin line of crimson. *Iron.*

Jack's hands flexed at his sides, seeming to try and draw magic, but failing.

"So, your magic is with nature? You reek of it." Tik-Tok only smirked. "Useful. But not right now."

While on the ship, Ozma had gone over the spells in her head, memorizing the words. There was one she could possibly use here, but only if his eyes focused on hers. It would be like holding his true name, ready for her to command him. Mombi had used it on her before but it only lasted moments, so the witch had found it worthless. It could buy them time here, though. Tik-Tok's burning red irises finally met hers, and she whispered the spell, urging him to obey her.

"Look at you." Tik-Tok smiled vengefully, exposing his back teeth. "Your pathetic spells aren't going to work on me. I'm protected. *So,* what are you going to do, darling?"

"He's not going to do it," Jack ground out. "If he were going to slit my throat, he would've done it already."

Ozma's eyes bulged, silently telling Jack to shut up. Even with Mombi, he'd never held his tongue, and that only made things worse.

"He's right, but my patience has its limits." Tik-Tok's red gaze bored into Ozma and he licked his lower lip. "I want to know why you're here first. Then, if I like what I hear, I may offer you a trade."

Tik-Tok didn't seem like one to be trusted, but with a blade at Jack's throat and a protection spell, what choice did she have? "Aren't you on the Wizard's side?"

"I'm on my own side. And, right now, it doesn't appear advantageous to help you." He cocked his head, his dark, sleek hair shifting forward. "Here's your chance to change my mind."

Ozma tilted her head right back at him, even though fear still pulsed through her veins for Jack. "One of my friends has taken back the South and the West in the Land of Oz, while another is in the process of redeeming the North and the East."

"How sweet," Tik-Tok purred. "But why would I give a fuck when I spend a majority of my time on the water, owned by no one." His blade dug into Jack harder, making her lover wince.

"Even if you kill us, our friends will come to end the Wizard, and I don't think you'll want to be on their bad side—which is exactly what will happen if you harm me." Ozma caught a glint of something gold at his wrist, where his gloved hand gripped the knife, beneath the fading sun. "We're here to reclaim Oz and stop the Wizard's darkness from spreading."

"I'm not sure his darkness *can* be stopped. Why fight a battle you can't win? It's much easier to join the winning side."

Ozma wondered what had made him decide to be a part of this. The money? Was he more than a pirate? A mercenary?

"She's the rightful queen of all of Oz," Jack interrupted, and Ozma glared at him. "You should be bowing down to her."

"Is she now?" Tik-Tok's gaze flicked up and down her body, as though starved for something—power.

"I am." Ozma lifted her chin, though she was frustrated with Jack for revealing her true identity to an enemy. But perhaps it was better this way, possibly an advantage. "The Wizard is only human, so even if we weren't to kill him, he'd eventually die of old age anyway."

"Is that what you think, darling?" Tik-Tok chuckled deeply, beautifully, viciously. "Not with the slippers. He's immortal now."

Ozma took a deep swallow, because she'd known he wanted to live forever. She'd known Mombi had been making him darker spells. That day he'd shown up at the witch's hut, he'd been wearing the slippers, but she hadn't known they'd been a part of the spell to make him immortal. "Mombi's dead. We killed her, and we'll do the same to him."

"Good. I never liked the bitch." He shrugged. "It's not as though the Wizard needs her now anyway."

Before Ozma could respond, Tik-Tok shoved Jack to the side. Instead of moving toward her, Jack stood frozen. An oddly dull texture—the color of slate gray—seeped up his skin, hardening him to stone. A statue.

"What did you do to him?" Ozma spat, keeping her voice low as not to alert anyone or any*thing*. She ran up to Jack and placed her hands against his rough cheeks, begging his worried expression to move. "Come on, Jack!"

"He's a distraction." Tik-Tok was suddenly behind her, his breath at her ear. "But don't worry, he can hear everything we say, see everything we do. And if you try to harm me, I won't change him back."

Ozma pushed the pirate away, her gaze catching on the gold of his wrist again—his skin was *metal*. "What happened to your arm?"

"It was a gift." He clenched his jaw and tugged his sleeve down. "Now, hand me your satchel."

She slowly removed the strap over her head and tossed the bag at his face.

He caught her satchel before it struck his nose. With a smile, he leaned his back against Jack's statue and motioned a finger at her to come closer. "Join me."

"No." She watched as he undid the clasp to her bag. "So that's your magic? Turning things to stone?" It seemed like a useful power—one she wished she had.

"I can do a lot of things."

"Then why didn't you stop us before?"

"I prefer to watch. But then I was impressed, and it wasn't hard to sniff you two out. I have a wicked sense of smell that's very useful in finding whomever I want." His nostrils flared when he inhaled. "You smell as though you have *no* magic."

Damn it. She couldn't even pretend to have power if she wanted to. "The Wizard is absorbing my magic. For the time being."

As if he wasn't listening, Tik-Tok slipped his hand into her satchel and started flipping through it. He tossed things to the ground, piece-by-piece, like they held no value. Loose papers flew through the air, fruit rolled across the grass. He lifted something up, glinting red, and stared at the heart-shaped stone that Ozma had taken from Mombi's cloak after Jack had killed her.

Tik-Tok arched a dark brow. "This can be part of the trade."

"Why ask? Couldn't you just take it?"

"I could."

"Fine." What did it matter? She didn't know what it was used for anyway. Linked to Mombi for protection? A magical amplifier?

"The Wizard refuses to return an object that belongs to me, hence why I'm open to other deals. I will help *Jack* get what is needed to break into the Wizard's house, then give you something that will allow you to share your lover's magic, but that's all. If the Wizard kills you both, I'll do nothing to save you."

"Why haven't you turned the Wizard to stone?" Perhaps she could find a way to persuade him to do just that.

Tik-Tok tossed the stone up, caught it, and tucked it into his pocket. "Oh, darling, my magic won't work against him. It was part of my trade with Mombi."

"And what was it you traded?"

He rested the back of his head against the stone of Jack and peered up at the sky. "That's rather irrelevant now that she's dead, don't you think?"

Ozma wasn't going to press further—he wasn't going to answer anyway. "What is it you want from me, then? A palace? Money?"

"I didn't know you had either of those things before I approached you, did I?" He pushed off Jack and took a step toward her, arms crossed. "There's a prophecy about a female with silver hair and dark eyes who hasn't been born yet. She'll be able to open portals through the sea. I will take her when I say it's time, and you will allow it. The female wouldn't be of your blood."

"Why would I let you kidnap some poor female?" she scoffed, knowing what it was like to be trapped herself.

"Yes? No? Or we're done here." There was a finality in his tone, and she knew she wouldn't be able to question anything else.

This was tricky. Too tricky. On one hand, Ozma would be sacrificing an innocent's life. On the other, she could potentially save the entirety of Oz by agreeing to this bargain. Images of Reva and Thelia slid into her mind, as did the few other good fae she'd met along the way. To save them all, she would have to agree to the deal. Even though she didn't know what he would do with the female, or with access to the portals.

"I agree." She pursed her lips, not knowing if she truly did the right thing. But it was the right thing to do in that moment. As a queen, she would have to make many more difficult decisions.

Tik-Tok waved his hand in the air, and a scratching sound came from Jack, like rocks rubbing together. The gray stone across his skin faded lighter and lighter until his flesh was pale and soft once more.

Jack stirred, and a choking noise came from his throat. Ozma started for him when Tik-Tok grabbed her by the arm, turning her to face him.

"Now"—he grinned—"it's your turn to rest while I chat with Jack."

Ozma's heart raced as his meaning sunk in. She opened her mouth to protest, finding her body unable to move, and seeing a gray hue spreading across her skin in the periphery of her vision. Everything around her grew heavier and heavier until she was completely still.

Chapter Twenty-Two

Jack

Jack's body slowly loosened from being a statue, but his mind raced. His heart was beating hard enough to bruise his ribs as his lungs strained to pull in enough oxygen. He'd seen and heard everything, but watching Ozma darken into stone was the worst part. It felt like his future was fading along with her body. He wanted to scream, to cry, to lash out and save her. But there was nothing he could do. His joints were still stuck, his voice still trapped.

Tik-Tok turned toward him and smirked. "Almost there, sunshine."

I'll destroy you, you cocky piece of shit!

Jack's fingers twitched. Then feeling flooded up his arms. The second his shoulders tensed, proving he had full range of motion, he swung a fist. It connected with Tik-Tok's jaw with a *thud.* His head snapped to the side from the impact and Jack rubbed his aching knuckles. "Bring her back." Jack commanded the vines to hold Tik-Tok captive, but they only swirled and moved around close by, none touching him.

Tik-Tok chuckled as he rubbed his face. When he looked

back at Jack, he licked a drop of blood from the corner of his lips and smiled. "So much fire in you. I *like* it. Now, put the vines down. I'm protected from that too."

Jack dropped his magic, lunged forward, and fisted Tik-Tok's shirt in his hands. "Son of a bitch! Bring Ozma back!"

"Now, now," he said calmly. "First, my mother *was* in fact a bitch so that isn't exactly an insult. And second, the same rule applies to you as it did to Ozma. Try to hurt me again and she remains an ornament."

Jack instantly released him and stepped back. As much as he wanted to beat the hell out of Tik-Tok, he couldn't do that to Ozma. *And I'm also a lousy fighter.* Another perk of being stuck on a farm his entire life. What had he punched? Pumpkins? They never swung back, and this foe looked like he fought everything that moved.

"Pity." Tik-Tok smoothed his shirt out. "She's quite lovely to look at. I could've tucked her in the corner of the captain's quarters to liven the place up a bit."

Jack bared his teeth.

"Calm your bits. No harm will come to your queen if you behave." His red eyes flashed with humor. "I'm one male and the two of you aren't trustworthy. This is easier. There will be no colluding behind my back or having to choose who to chase down if you run in different directions."

"Easier for you," Jack snarled. As far as he knew, Tik-Tok didn't realize how terrifying it was to become stone. It was as if his whole body had seized up, the air slowly squeezed from his lungs.

He shrugged. "*Meh.* It doesn't matter. Let's get moving."

Jack turned, following the pirate's nonchalant movements. "We can't just *leave* her here like this."

"Why not? It's not as if the fiends can eat her like that." He didn't even bother glancing over his shoulder as he spoke. "Don't fall behind."

Jack stared helplessly at Ozma, her face frozen in shock. He wanted to wipe the fear away with a kiss as he always did, but there would be no changing her expression until she was no longer stone.

"Chop, chop!" came Tik-Tok's voice from farther away.

"I love you," he told the statue, cupping her cool stone cheeks. "I'll be back as soon as I can. I swear." Then he raced after the bastard.

Jack felt the distance between himself and Ozma grow as he caught up to the other male. It was a tangible weight, pulling him back. Leaving her out in the open with so many monsters prowling felt wrong. Just because they hadn't followed them all the way to the Wizard, that didn't mean they wouldn't eventually wander that way.

She's stone, he reminded himself. The asshole was right—they wouldn't want to eat her. *Couldn't.* But what if something else happened? An animal or one of those addicts could accidentally knock her over. What if she broke? *Would* she break? He'd felt pretty solid when he was frozen…

It was getting darker by the minute. For all he knew, there were other dangerous fae lurking about. If he and Tik-Tok were attacked and something happened to either of them, what would become of Ozma?

"I give you my word that no harm will come to Ozma," Tik-Tok said in a sincere tone. Jack hadn't known he was capable of speaking that way. Then the fae clapped his hands together and smirked. "Now. Focus."

Focus. I'll focus … on how to kill you the second Ozma is back.

"You said the Wizard has something of yours," Jack said, recalling Tik-Tok's conversation with Ozma.

"Not for much longer. That's what you're for."

"What is it?" Jack asked with a scowl.

"An enchanted object."

He leveled a stare at the back of Tik-Tok's head. "You don't say."

"I'd prefer to say *nothing* until we get there," he replied casually, but the implication was clear. *Shut the fuck up.*

Jack balled his hands into fists. He would listen, not because he was afraid of the fae, but because Ozma's life depended on it. If he were being honest, Tik-Tok's plan was smart. Put one of them in danger to guarantee the other behaves. *Fucking asshole.* He bit his tongue and trudged farther into the woods.

Orkland wasn't a huge island judging by the maps he'd seen, but that was in comparison to all of Oz. It could take days to cross it for all Jack knew. It had taken one just to find the Wizard, but there was no telling how far from the other coasts they were.

The longer they walked, the worse the forest became. The skeletal trees with dripping fruit slowly lessened. In their place stood rotting stumps covered in black sludge. Each stump was hollow except for more stagnant goop, and the bark that was left clinging to the outside protruded in jagged strips. Tiny flies floated, dead, on the surface.

The ground was soggy beneath Jack's boots, and he'd never been so glad of his worn footwear. With the sun nearly gone, Tik-Tok hurried his pace, causing the thick liquid to splash up onto their pant legs.

In front of him, Tik-Tok kicked something from his path. A skull skidded across the ground in front of Jack, cracked and covered in muck, with pointed teeth.

Fucking hell.

There would be no getting this stench out—especially if it was partially made of dead bodies. He would have to burn his clothes after this. Perhaps it was better that he wouldn't be able to see much going forward. He could pretend the ground was made of fertilizer after a heavy rain and the smell was simply rotting pumpkins. Nothing new there.

"Your power is rather handy," Tik-Tok said conversationally, breaking the silence that had lasted uncomfortably long. He slowed to walk beside Jack instead of in front of him. "Can you do anything else?"

Jack shrugged. He wasn't aware fae regularly had multiple

abilities, but if they did, he wanted to find out what else he was capable of. *Later.*

"Hmm." Tik-Tok's eyes practically glowed with the last rays of sunlight. "It's a new power for you—that's why you exhausted it so quickly—so maybe you'll come into more later. You're young yet."

"Not that young," Jack grumbled.

"No? A decade past maturity, I'd guess."

Accurate, you kelpie scum. "It's really none of your business."

"I'm approaching my first century now. By the time I was your age, I had at least three abilities. My first was feeling weather before it happened—quite useful on the sea. Then I—"

"What happened to not talking?" Jack snapped. He *was* curious about what else this asshole fae could do, but he was more concerned with finishing their quest without attracting any of the rotting creatures.

"You piqued my curiosity, but fine. That's our destination." He pointed to the lone silhouette of a tree.

It was free of both fruit and leaves, its branches reaching skyward in perfectly straight angles. As they approached, Tik-Tok took an orb from the pouch at his waist. It lit up in his palm, casting them and the immediate area in a soft white glow. The orb highlighted the razor-sharp edges of the branches and the rough, gritty texture of the bark. The tree was variegated brown and white instead of solid black like the ones on the rest of the island.

"Okay," Jack said slowly.

Tik-Tok motioned to a round knot jutting from the middle of the trunk. "Use your magic to open this and take the object inside."

Jack crossed his arms. Telling him how low his powers were seemed like a fucking horrible idea. The pirate had implied that he knew Jack was running low, but not *this* low. He wouldn't be able to defend himself for long if anything went wrong, but why give him the advantage of *knowing* that? "Why can't you do it?

Hack at it with an axe or something."

"Hack at it with an axe," he repeated mockingly. "As if I haven't spent years trying to crack it open? Oz spelled it against me and my crew specifically to ensure my loyalty."

"Why does it feel like it's better to leave this thing where it is?" *Because it probably is.*

"It's mine," Tik-Tok said through a false smile. "And I want it back."

Jack hesitated. The enemy of his enemy wasn't his friend … but they could be temporary allies. Whether he was lying about the object or not wasn't important. They needed to kill Oz, then get the hell off this island. Not that he had much choice in helping if he wanted Ozma safe.

"And the thing inside will get us into Oz's house?" Jack asked.

"It will," he replied with a stiff nod.

Jack licked his lips. There should be enough magic for the task, but he wasn't sure how much would be left to fight the Wizard afterward. Especially if he had to share it with Ozma—however that worked. But no one would be fighting Oz if they couldn't *get* to him. Jack sighed and lifted his arm.

Open.

The knot struggled to obey. Maybe he needed to be more specific. Instead of using words, he imagined the knot peeling back. The edges unfurling. The center flaking away. And, this time, the tree listened. Inside, a glint of gold sparkled with the light Tik-Tok held.

"Take it," he urged.

Jack stepped closer and carefully plucked the octagonal piece from its hiding place. It was large enough to fill his palm, no thicker than the shell of a regular-sized pumpkin, and surprisingly light.

Tik-Tok held out his free hand. "Give it to me."

Jack turned it over to the other male and watched him carefully for a reaction. The pirate clutched the object tightly with his gloved hands, held it to his lips, and whispered inaudibly. Jack only knew he spoke because his lips moved. And then the object popped open.

Tik-Tok grinned wildly. "It still works."

Jack leaned forward and caught a glimpse of the needle spinning around inside. The face was marked with North, South, East, and West, with tiny scores around the outer edge. "A compass? How will that get us into Oz's house?"

"This isn't just any compass," he said in awe. "It's *my* compass."

Jack lifted a brow. "And that means…?"

Tik-Tok shot him an irritated look. "Never mind. Let's get back to your precious Ozma and I'll keep my word to get you in to see the Wizard."

"Wonderful," Jack said flatly. His muscles ached and his body felt void of any magic. Completely tapped of energy in general. When had they last gotten a decent night's rest? When had they eaten? It felt like a lifetime ago. But there was no way he was going to delay the return trip.

Not when Ozma was in torment inside her stone body.

Chapter Twenty-Three

Ozma

The dark night wrapped around Ozma's stone flesh, and the stars shone through slits in the trees, allowing her to see straight ahead. It was strange, not being able to move, yet somehow still feeling the wind blowing against her. In the dark place, Reva had spoken of gnomes made entirely out of rock—was this what they felt? Their nerves still coming alive beneath hardened flesh?

Time passed and passed as she worried about Jack, wondering if Tik-Tok would betray him. Even though the pirate seemed like a selfish prick, she prayed he wouldn't harm Jack.

Finally, as night bugs swarmed past her, the sound of footsteps and leaves crunching echoed, interrupting her thoughts as they drew closer. If she could hold her breath any more than her stone lungs were already doing, Ozma would have done so. She hoped it wasn't fae or humans from the swarm. She relaxed when a flash of orange hair appeared in the silver of the moonlight, followed by Tik-Tok's dark mane.

The pirate stroked the sword at his hip and sauntered toward Ozma. "Wake up, darling." He flicked his hand in the air, and a sizzling noise sounded in her head as her skin became lighter, freer. Her body jerked forward, feet stumbling, until Jack's hands wrapped around her waist, catching her.

"Are you all right?" he whispered, his hazel gaze holding hers.

"I'm fine," she choked out, her voice raspy. Ozma's throat felt scratchy as she took a deep swallow, then another.

A twig snapped behind her. Ozma withdrew her dagger and whirled around.

Tik-Tok lifted a brow and bit into one of the fruits he'd tossed from her satchel earlier. "Sorry, did you want this back?" he asked, slowly chewing with a smirk.

Ozma released a frustrated sigh and focused on Jack. "Did he retrieve what we needed to get inside?" She didn't know what exactly it was the pirate had gone to find. He could have been lying when he'd said that the object would allow them access to see the Wizard.

Jack ran a hand through his hair, his eyes sliding to Tik-Tok. "So he says."

"I'm wounded you still don't trust me." Tik-Tok took another bite of the fruit, then fished out something golden from his pocket. "It will work." She only caught a glimpse of its octagonal shape before he pressed it back into his pants.

Jack ignored Tik-Tok and knelt on the ground. He plucked up the last couple pieces of their fruit, then tossed her a plum. "We'll need some strength before we try to go in."

Ozma sank her teeth into the sweet fruit and peered up at the full moon mounted in the sky, the constellations of stars clustered together, and the small wings of night creatures pumping across the treetops. "Should we wait until morning?" she asked, not knowing if the time of day would really make a difference.

"The fiends can find you more easily at night," Tik-Tok started. "Their sight works better in the dark, so I say move now. Kill Oz when he's least expecting it."

The Wizard would most likely be asleep, and perhaps there

were a way she could catch him easily, then cut his throat. But if he wasn't asleep… "What about sharing magic with Jack? How are you going to make that happen?" Ozma needed something more than a dagger and a few spells that wouldn't even work against the Wizard.

Tik-Tok grinned secretively, and tugged off his glove, revealing a hand made entirely of gold. The color was an exact match to the object he'd flashed her a moment ago. His hand appeared to be a real appendage, and as he flexed his fingers, she noticed it even moved like one. The only differences aside from the coloring were the tiny screws in areas where the joints bent, and the overlapping folds that could be seen when he shifted his digits and wrist. She couldn't see how far the metal stretched up, and if it was his entire arm—or only to the elbow.

Thin silver rings with jewels of different hues decorated all of his fingers, except for one in the middle that was entirely of silver. "I don't give anything away lightly. Or at all." He removed the silver ring from his middle finger and held it up in front of her face. It shone brightly as if flecked with glitter. "I'll want it back when I collect the female."

Ozma reached to grab it, but he delicately moved her hand away. "No." He bit his lower lip. "Give me your hand. It has to be transferred with freewill."

"Hold on—" Jack interrupted, anger lacing his words as he stepped in front of Ozma. "What kind of sick game are you playing? You aren't going to place that damn thing on her finger, then say she's your wife."

"If I didn't already have plans for another, she would do well," Tik-Tok purred. "But your queen is safe from such things."

Jack's hands clenched at his sides and Ozma pulled him back beside her. As she took a deep swallow, her stomach sank at the thought of the unknown fae belonging to this male in the future. Straightening her spine and lifting her chin, she placed her hand into his anyway. His cool metal fingertips gently held her as he slid the silver circle onto her middle digit. The ring was loose at first, but it tightened around her finger, the color changing from silver to gold, by some sort of magic.

She went to twist it to the side, to examine, but the ring wouldn't budge. Ozma's eyes widened, her heart accelerating as her gaze darted from Jack to Tik-Tok. "What did you do?" Her voice shot up an octave.

"It will stay on. Even years from now, the ring will remain there, until our agreement is complete. But it will also allow you to share another's magic as long as they are without a protection spell. Just study whom you want to borrow from while whispering, 'divide one's magic and make it as though mine,' to ignite it."

Ozma whispered the words, while staring at Jack, and something stirred within her. *Magic.* It didn't feel attached to her, though. The power seemed to be floating, and perhaps this would make it so the Wizard couldn't absorb that from her too. Lifting her arm, she studied a vine above and twisted her hand. She squinted and focused on it to move until the vine slowly slithered forward, its pointed end curling.

"Where did you get this from?" Ozma asked, releasing the vine, pushing it back into its original place. She wanted to use more of the power, test it, but would hold off until inside Oz's home.

"One of the sea witches gave me the ring as a gift to assist with the prophecy. I did have to fuck her to keep it, but she's a good female. Like you." Tik-Tok reached for a lock of her hair and Jack slapped his hand away.

"Stop trying to touch her," Jack seethed, narrowing his eyes.

"Perhaps"—Tik-Tok's smirk grew wicked with delight—"two females in the future might suit me better than one. What do you think, darling?" His fiery, red gaze lit with playfulness. He didn't even glance at Jack.

"Quit toying with Jack when we've already made a deal," Ozma said.

"That wasn't necessarily a *never*. But don't worry, Jack. You did a good deed for me, so I'll leave you your queen." Tik-Tok chuckled and motioned them forward. "Come on then. I'll help you get past the Wizard's barrier."

"Why don't you just give us the compass," Jack grunted as he walked beside Ozma through the forest.

"How about … I give you nothing?" Tik-Tok peered over his shoulder with a smirk, sliding his glove back on and flexing his fingers. Ozma wondered what it would be like to have a metal arm, one that still moved just the same. Could he feel with it?

Loud chirping noises echoed as the trio traveled further, the moonlight guiding their way down twisting paths. The area was bright enough to see their shadows reflecting across the moistened dirt and grass, along with the outlines of trees and shriveled branches. As they drew closer, she could see a flickering of green flashing into the sky, emanating from the Wizard's home.

In the distance, growls and rustling stirred, but they weren't near enough for Ozma to be worried, although her heart still pounded ferociously. She also knew Jack was running low on magic, so she hoped whatever creatures were out there stayed where they were.

As they approached the Wizard's house, the emerald light glistened even more in the darkness, like a beacon. The swarm didn't sound any nearer, their noises remaining in the distance.

As they came to the edge of the barrier, Ozma halted, but Tik-Tok pressed his metal arm forward, and the barrier didn't stop him. His fingers brushed a wooden pole and pushed something. A hidden button? Around the Wizard's sanctuary, the barrier flickered once, twice, then vanished, as if it had never been there at all.

"It helps to have a metal arm," he cooed.

"So I suppose you didn't really need the compass to get us in here," Jack grunted.

A shuffling came from the back of the house, then a figure

rounded it, slipping into view. Before Ozma could draw magic from Jack, a dagger sailed past her from behind and planted itself into the guard's head. His knees buckled, and his body folded to the ground with a thud.

"Looky there, you don't have to worry about the guard now," Tik-Tok said.

Ozma frowned but took a step forward at the same time Jack did. She'd thought that maybe an invisible barrier would still be there, yet they passed through unharmed. With a glance over her shoulder, she noticed Tik-Tok hadn't moved.

Tik-Tok reached into his pocket and tugged out his object. While cradling it, he brought it to his mouth and whispered something in another language. The object shifted, as though alive, unfolding until she recognized it as a compass. The dial in the center glowed a pale gold as it started spinning around and around.

"Are you coming?" she whispered.

"No." He shook his head. "I'm headed for my ship. My crew will leave a rowboat on shore for you. If you're still alive, use it by dawn to get back on board. Otherwise, we'll retrieve the boat and you'll be trapped, as I won't be coming back." With those words, he turned around, striding straight toward the sounds of the horde in the distance, leaving Ozma and Jack alone once more.

This time, to face the Wizard.

Chapter Twenty-Four

Jack

Before Jack knew it, Tik-Tok had strutted out of sight. A portion of Jack's power had transferred to Ozma, leaving him feeling slightly weakened, and they were alone inside the barrier with a dead guard. Unless Oz counted—in which case, it was hopefully only him, Ozma, and a soon-to-be-dead immortal. *Fucking insanity.* Were they really doing this? The most dangerous thing he'd fought before Ozma returned from the dark place were stubborn weeds. Now they were about to face *the most dangerous being in Oz.* Stealing Ozma's power had made the Wizard that way, but unless they could revert the magic to her, there was little hope of winning.

"Ozma," he said, his voice shaking slightly.

She looked up at him with her large blue eyes, and he saw his own fear reflected there. "We'll be all right. We just have to get the slippers and everything else will work out."

That seemed overly simplistic, but there was no turning back now. "I suppose, we're off to kill the Wizard, then," he said with forced lightness.

Ozma nodded and, together, they crept closer to the house.

The outer walls were made of black wood, assumably from the surrounding trees, but the rounded door and shutters were painted emerald green. Only faint candlelight burned through the windows and no smoke billowed from the chimney, despite the growing chill in the air.

Every step Jack took beside Ozma felt like it would be his last. A trap would spring, or an alarm would go off, and then it would all be over. So, when they made it up to the house without incident, it was almost too good to be true.

Ozma stretched up onto her toes and peered into the window. Jack's scant meal from earlier threatened to reappear. *Don't see us,* he prayed as he joined her at the glass. *Please don't fucking see us.*

Inside, light filtered into a living room from the hallway. A rug was rolled up beside an unlit fireplace and most of the furniture was covered with white sheets. An overstuffed brown couch and a dark, low table were the only things exposed. Papers were scattered across the table beside a glass half-full of amber liquid.

A small vine had managed to flatten completely and work its way into a narrow crack under the windowsill, with the help of Jack's power via Ozma. He'd barely felt the small trickle of magic pass to her. The vine unwrapped itself from the latch now that it was open, and slithered back to the flowerbox.

"It's unlocked now," Ozma said with a proud smirk. She placed her palms on the window and slid it upward. To Jack's surprise, it didn't stick or creak.

"We can't just crawl in through the window," he hissed.

Ozma shot him a perplexed look. "Why not? It's not like we haven't done it a thousand times before."

A smile tugged at Jack's lips but didn't fully form. It was true—they'd both snuck out of the window in Jack's cabin more times than he could remember—but the consequences were very different. Mombi would beat them for disobedience or possibly make them go hungry for a day or two, but the Wizard would kill them. At least, he would kill Jack.

Jack took Ozma's face in his hands and pressed a desperate, wild kiss to her lips. He drank her in as if she were the last breath of a dying male, which was possibly true. She returned the kiss with equal vigor, but broke away too soon, panting.

"We'll finish *that* later," she promised. Then, without waiting for him to agree to her plan, she slipped easily through the open window. Jack scrambled in behind her less gracefully but just as silent.

Over the pounding of his own heart, a cheerful hum carried through the room. It was slightly muffled by the walls but became clearer the closer it came. He quickly darted behind a covered settee with Ozma right beside him. They hid not a moment too soon as the chandelier flashed magically above the center of the room. Two flashes later and the candles remained lit, casting the room in ghostly white light.

Now what? he mouthed.

Ozma held a finger to her lips and peered between a gap in the furniture as someone walked into the room. A gasp left her lips a moment later and she slapped a hand over her mouth at the tiny sound. *That's a fucking great sign.* What had she seen, *exactly*? He wasn't in a position to look without being caught and he couldn't very well ask her.

The humming hit a crescendo before ending abruptly in favor of a soft *thump* followed by a loud yawn. "Right, right, right," the Wizard mumbled to himself. His voice sounded different than Jack remembered. Less raspy. *Was* it the Wizard? Or perhaps another guard?

"Where was I?" he continued with a shuffle of papers.

Ozma tapped Jack's knee and, when he looked at her, she motioned beneath the settee. There was a decent sized gap between the cloth and the floorboards. Jack eased himself down to his hands and knees and peered beneath.

In front of the brown couch were two feet.

And on those feet, the silver slippers.

The material sparkled with every small movement the Wizard made. They hugged his feet tightly, showcasing large bunions that stretched the sides outward, and the flat soles tapped on the bare floor with a soft *tick, tick, tick*. It *had* to be him if he wore the slippers—there was no chance he would allow anyone else to put them on. Ozma nudged Jack's knee again and made a cutting motion with two fingers.

She … wanted to cut the slippers from the Wizard? Even if it were possible to cut the shoes, it would ruin them. She needed their magic to get her power back—and her wings.

Seeming to sense his confusion, Ozma made the cutting motion again, this time against his ankle. Was she serious? Cut his *feet* off? Why not simply kill him and take the shoes from his corpse? It seemed safer. Though, he supposed, in order to kill Oz, they needed to strip him of his power first. Which meant slippers first, death second.

Just fucking great.

Ozma nudged him gently with her elbow.

Jack pointed to his chest, silently asking *me?*

Magic, she mouthed.

His mind raced over what he could possibly do with his magic to *cut someone's feet off*. Even if any plants were inside, it would take far too long to squeeze through flesh and bone with a vine. Surely someone as powerful as Oz would have a way to stop them if given even a moment's chance. Killing him first was really the better option.

Jack held Ozma's stare and slid a finger across his throat. Not that he cared if they slit his throat, set him on fire, or poured poison down his throat. The bastard just needed to die.

Ozma bit her lip and nodded. After a moment's hesitation, his magic tugged in his veins as she drew out part of his power. Her eyes narrowed in concentration and a drop of sweat rolled down her temple. Whatever she was doing, it was big. Jack could feel the life of the plants outside swell within him.

"I know you're there," the Wizard said suddenly.

Ozma's concentration faltered and Jack's heart tripped over itself.

"If you're going to sneak in, you might want to close the window next time."

Fuck. Fuck fuck fuck fuck fuck.

Oz heaved an agitated sigh. "Your foolishness is growing old, Tik-Tok. The compass is yours once the Land of Oz is secured as mine."

He thinks we're Tik-Tok. Relief flooded over Jack in waves, but, as each wave receded, terror screamed through him again. They weren't Tik-Tok, but they were still caught. If they didn't make their move *now*, it would be too late.

Jack squeezed Ozma's hand, her palm slick against his. She returned the motion, then slipped free of his grasp.

And stood.

"Sorry to disappoint you," she said in a level voice. If Jack didn't know her so well, he wouldn't have noticed the small tremor. "The pirate ran back to his ship."

"Ozma," the Wizard growled. "How the hell did you get here?"

She flicked her hand at Jack behind the settee as if telling him to hurry, then she stepped away. Closer to Oz. "It's a long story, though you may find it interesting."

Jack crawled to where Ozma had previously sat and looked through the same crack she had. It was indeed the Wizard of Oz. Only, it wasn't.

The man Jack had seen picking up Mombi's spells at the farm had white hair, age spots, and rotting teeth. Plus, the gleam in his eyes had looked absolutely insane. But this … this human was in his early twenties at most. Carefully coiffed dark hair set off his pale, porcelain skin and perfect white teeth. His full lips had dropped in shock—and maybe a little in awe of Ozma's return—though his blazing green eyes showed only fury.

"In the dark place"—Ozma began—"I met Reva. The Wicked Witch of the West, as you likely remember her, though she wasn't wicked at all. Or maybe she was. She *did* teach me all sorts of ways to kill."

She's distracting him. Jack swallowed hard at the realization and scrambled to come up with a plan. Slippers… He needed the slippers. *Think, Jack!*

"That bitch survived eight years on her own?" Oz said with a surprised laugh.

"And two with me."

The Wizard leaned into the settee, resting his arms on the back as if Ozma's presence wasn't a threat. "What a triumphant return you've made," he said in a flat voice.

"Our return is credited to Dorothy Gale—or Thelia, as her parents named her."

The Wizard's face drained of what little color it had.

"But, regardless of the method, I wouldn't exactly call our return triumphant." Ozma licked her lips and stalked a bit closer. "Not yet, anyway."

Jack wanted to leap out and pull Ozma away from him. She was too close. The Wizard could lunge at her, throw a potion … anything, really. His magic throbbed as Ozma tapped into it again. A message to hurry. He wished there were more of his magic to spare…

Fuck it.

Immobilize the ass, then worry about the slippers.

With a single blast of power, Jack plucked the thorn off every un-pruned rosebush outside and sent them sailing through the window. Once in the room, he forced more magic at them, doubling each thorn's size. Tripling them. They instinctively flew around Ozma, aiming straight for the Wizard's chest.

"What the fuck is this?" the Wizard shouted.

Oz was on his feet, his hands thrown outward toward the incoming thorns. Ozma ripped into Jack's magic supply, painfully gouging out almost every ounce he had left, and the floor buckled beneath them.

A black, jagged tree burst upward and didn't stop until it

broke through the ceiling. Branches speared outward at nearly every angle. One sliced through Jack's thigh and he let out a strangled cry. If it weren't for the Wizard's own scream, it would've given him away. He grimaced through the pain and looked up to find a large branch had struck through Oz's left shoulder. It pinned him to the far wall like an insect.

"This isn't your magic," Oz shouted between painful gasps. "Where's the slave hiding?"

Ah. So he was exposed either way.

Jack struggled to his feet, blood flowing freely from the wide gash in his leg. "I'm no slave, *mortal.*"

"Young love." Oz smiled a wicked smile. A smile that promised something. "Once a slave, always a slave, eh? Though your master is admittedly better looking this time."

Ozma quickly drew the dagger from her belt and gripped the handle so hard her knuckles turned white. Who was Jack to stop her if she wanted to hack away at the Wizard's feet before Oz was dead? It wasn't like Oz didn't deserve it. In the scheme of things, he was getting off easy. Still, his gut churned. This was *too* easy…

Oz slapped his open palm to the wall behind him and green light exploded through the room.

Chapter Twenty-Five

Ozma

Ozma screamed and dropped to her knees as the green illumination around her grew brighter and brighter. Sharp pain lanced her right eye, and her vision went black on that side. Her wailing ended as she lifted her hand and felt warm blood leaking down her cheek. Fingers shaking, she brushed against a hard object planted in her eye. With quick motions, Ozma ripped it out and released a cry. The room spun, her head dizzy, and she heaved.

Her gaze settled on one of the thorns that Jack had sent riveting into the Wizard's home. Somehow, when the Wizard threw his green light back, it must have sent some of the thorns soaring again, piercing her eye.

The emerald light remained bright, flickering across the room, against the large tree that had exploded in the room with Jack's power. Her uninjured eye could only squint in the intense brightness.

Ozma dropped the thorn and felt around the hard flooring to get to Jack. She crawled forward, widening her good eye as the light around her dimmed a fraction. Two hands wrapped around Ozma's neck, lifting her by the throat, then shoved her against a wall. The room cleared of green and the stark white light returned. She met the cold emerald eyes of the Wizard. There wasn't a single wrinkle or blackened tooth on him. The shock of discovering him this way—so different—still hadn't worn off. No longer withering, but young and full of life. Like he must have been when he'd first come to the Land of Oz. This had to be the reason Mombi had appeared frailer than ever—she was using more and more dark magic to restore his youth, while the shoes and Ozma's power had been making him immortal. Even the wound where Jack had struck him with the tree appeared to be healing.

"Ozma, you beautiful thing," Oz said pleasantly, his body firmly against hers. "Aren't you wondering why I haven't sent you back to the black pit yet? Did you really think I didn't know you were attempting to distract me earlier? I knew exactly what you were doing."

She had wondered it, but she wasn't going to start asking. Instead, she whispered a spell that would make Oz obey her, but all he did was cluck his tongue at her. Tik-Tok hadn't been lying about that—the Wizard *was* protected from spells. She moved to shove her dagger forward and he easily confiscated it, sliding it into the belt at his waist.

Oz tsked. "That wasn't very nice."

She would have to wait for the right time to get it back. "Where's Jack?" Ozma searched past Oz, around the room and the tree, the couch, the window, but she couldn't spot him anywhere. Why wasn't Jack taking the opportunity to attack the Wizard? Unless the thorns had done something worse to him, taken more than his eye. Her heart struck her rib cage and her stomach dropped at the thought.

"Your precious slave will make the perfect guest at our wedding." Oz's smile grew wide, his white teeth glistening from the chandelier's candlelight. "I just need to wait for Mombi to return so we can cast the spell to give her your body. The slippers' magic wouldn't have let you die from the dangers in that darkness."

Ozma's eyes widened in horror. "*What*?" Gritting her teeth, she tried to dip into Jack's magic, needing to find the power to draw forth a tree branch or vine, *anything*. But nothing stirred within her.

"You arrived sooner than expected." He pressed his nose to her hair and inhaled. "Mombi was supposed to get the remainder of her potions, summon you back to Oz herself, and bring you here."

"Mombi's dead." Ozma tried to wiggle out from his grasp, but he was pressed too tightly against her.

Oz's brows lifted, and his lips formed an O of surprise. "A pity we can't use your body for her now." He shrugged, staring hard at her. "But there's always another option, isn't there? You're still here." With motions too quick for a mortal, Oz spun her the other direction and squeezed his hands around her wrists behind her back, then walked her forward. "Let's get you dressed now."

"No," she shouted, kicking back at him.

Oz's other hand came to her throat, his fingers digging in at the sensitive area right under her jaw. He twisted her head to the side so her stare fell to a lump on the floor. A body of gnarled twigs with thin fingers and toes, and a pumpkin for a head. An emerald green leaf rested near the stem at the top of the pumpkin. As Ozma recognized the clothes the horrible creation wore, tears of anger burned down her cheeks. *Jack*.

"Fix him!" she screamed, wanting to claw at the Wizard, but his hold was too solid.

"I don't think so," he spat, tightening his grip even more as he pushed her forward into an open bedroom.

Spell books and jars filled with body parts were neatly placed on wooden shelves against the walls. It smelled of Mombi—her room. Two wooden wardrobes stood beside a bed on the opposite side of the room. A white gown lay sprawled over the mattress with hideous yellow jewels stitched into the bodice. Beside it rested a crown, sapphire and emerald jewels embedded in the gold.

An awful thought slammed into her. Mombi had been planning to use Ozma's body to reclaim the throne and ensure no one could take it from Oz in the future. Ozma knew Mombi hadn't been in love with Oz—she'd wanted power, most likely believed it was owed to her for all the help she'd given.

The Wizard thrust Ozma onto the mattress, taking her by surprise, and she flipped over to face him.

"Unless you want me to set fire to the slave, get dressed," Oz snapped, inching closer, the silver slippers alight with magic.

Ozma's heart thrummed frantically in her chest as she thought about the closeness of the Wizard, and about what had happened to Jack. "Why have me marry you? I won't obey you or help you rule Oz."

"Dear girl, is that what you think I'm still doing?" The Wizard released a loud chuckle, echoing maddeningly off the walls around her, his handsome face training on her with an ugly expression. "You're going to fuck me willingly so I can absorb your magic permanently. Then I'll free your slave."

Oz leaned forward and swiped a long finger slowly down her cheek, making her shudder. His digit came away coated with crimson from her wound, then he tenderly licked the blood clean from his fingertip. "Even with one eye, you'll make a pretty fuck, and I'm sure you'll taste as good as your magic."

Ozma held back another shiver. She wasn't going to put on that dress and let him press his cock inside her. Even if she did as he asked, Ozma knew he would never change Jack back. No matter how much she loved Jack, she couldn't do as Oz wanted. If the Wizard took whatever power she still had, he would use it to destroy everyone, including her and Jack.

Oz was protected from spells, but it was obvious by his shoulder wound that he could still be harmed.

"You promise to return Jack to his fae form?" Ozma

whispered.

"I will." He grinned savagely. "The last time I had a good fuck was Langwidere, and you'll need to make it better than that."

Closing her eyes, Ozma took a deep swallow. "Fine." She grabbed him by his collar and drew him close.

The Wizard was immortal now, appeared youthful, but no spell would take away the lingering scent of decay. Holding her breath, she pressed her lips to his and pulled him down on top of her. A low growl escaped his throat as he kissed her back, his lips devouring her. His lower body rocked into hers, and she could feel the swell of his length. With each movement of his mouth and each rolling of his hips, she yearned to murder him more, tear his body into pieces.

"Your sole purpose in this world was to belong to me. Your power was always meant to be mine," he cooed in her ear, then crashed his lips onto hers again, tasting, licking, probing. Repulsion washed over her as he lowered his hands between them to unbuckle his belt, and she fought the desire to rip off his cock.

This was the moment. She reached for the dagger at his hip and quickly drew it out. His eyes bulged, but he wasn't fast enough as she slashed a smile, reflecting her own, across his throat. A burst of magic knocked her back, holding her to the bed, as Oz choked on his own blood. She pushed through the power as Oz's magic seemed to weaken.

Ozma sat up, grabbed her dagger again, and lunged for the Wizard, knocking him to the floor. Bringing the weapon up, she plunged it into his throat.

He struggled for a few more moments, then his movements stopped, his breathing ceased, and any life that was in his eyes was now gone.

The Wizard might have been one of the most powerful individuals in Oz but that was only because of others. And behind all that glamour, he was still just a human male, thinking with his cock first.

Ozma's gaze settled at the slippers on his feet and she hurried to tear them away, but they wouldn't budge. She peered around Mombi's room for something she could use, but the witch had never kept weapons before. She didn't appear to now, either. If Ozma could only use the dagger to saw through Oz's bones, she would have, but the blade wasn't large or sharp enough.

Not wanting to take her eyes off the Wizard's body longer than she had to, she barreled out of the room and into the one beside it.

This room was messy, with notebooks and maps thrown everywhere. Rumpled blankets were clumped on a bed against the wall. Beside it was a nightstand with two emerald-jeweled swords resting against it. Buckets and buckets of faerie fruit, unlike the shriveled ones of Orkland's trees, were stored in a corner. Ozma ignored the sharper smell of decay, in what must have been the Wizard's room, as she snatched one of the weapons and darted back to where his body lay.

Oz was just the same—he hadn't roused back to life. Rapid healing wouldn't have helped with a fatal blow, but with Mombi's dark spells, she hadn't been sure.

Lifting the blade high, she swung it down across both ankles, severing them from the bastard.

A blast of something rocketed through Ozma, and she inhaled sharply. It was what rightfully belonged to her, what she'd only truly felt once. *Her* magic.

It spun and it spun within her, connecting to each nerve in her body, attaching to every inch of her. But, unlike before, feathery wings didn't emerge from her back.

Ozma dropped to her knees and picked up one of the Wizard's feet, removing the first blood-speckled slipper, and rushing to place it on her bare foot. It tightened around her flesh, then the dull silver lit up, like it had on Oz, and a pulse of magic stormed through her. Releasing the bloody foot, she grabbed the other one and ripped off the second slipper. She didn't care about cleaning the crimson right now—she slipped the shoe on, and it illuminated with bright flecks of silver.

Brushing off her dress, Ozma stood and turned to go to Jack but stopped when another blast of power ignited within her. A hard jab came at her back, then another, and another, as though something were pounding at a door behind her skin. As she reached to touch the throbbing scar, two pale blue wings shot through her flesh, ripping the back of her dress. The feathered wings folded around her as though hugging her.

Tears sprung from her eyes, because this was the part of herself she'd mourned the most. With a sigh, she smiled and drew them back into her body before sprinting out of the room toward Jack.

Nothing had changed with him since the Wizard's death. His head was still a pumpkin, his appendages thin sticks that could easily be snapped and broken for good. It had been Oz's power that had made him this way. But that wasn't right—it was *her* magic the Wizard had used. She should be able to change him back with that same power. *Please.* Cradling the outer shell of his head, Ozma murmured to him, "Jackseith Arel Diosyll, return to me."

Glittering blue smoke swarmed around her, spinning in a circle. Jack's body fidgeted, his stick hand squeezing hers. A muffled cry came from somewhere within the faceless pumpkin—Jack struggling to somehow speak.

Ozma's hands shook with fear, but then she realized what she'd done wrong. "Return to your fae form." Magic spilled out of her, wrapping around Jack like a blanket. The bluish color became a cloud of orange smoke.

The smoke vanished as though it had never been there at all, revealing hair the color of a morning sunrise, freckles across tan cheeks, pointed ears—*Jack.* Sweat glistened on his forehead as his lids snapped open.

"You're okay," she whispered, pressing a hand to his cheek. "Jackseith Arel Diosyll, I release you."

"I rather preferred being a stone statue," he rasped, slowly sitting up. Then his eyes widened as he focused on her. "Your eye!"

"It is what it is." Ozma softly kissed his lips, then pressed her forehead to his. "The Wizard's dead, and my magic and wings are back."

He wrapped his hands around her and hauled her into his lap. "I'm taking the bastard's head and feeding it to the wild fae in the forest. There's no way he'll ever come back from that."

Chapter Twenty-Six

Jack

Outside the Wizard's house, Jack took a moment to pat his hip to be sure his knife was still there. To return to the ship and get the hell out of Orkland, they would have to venture back through the swarm of rotting fae and humans. It wouldn't be possible to outrun them this time. Not when his leg was sliced open and they would be heading straight into the horde, which was why he clutched the Wizard's severed head in one hand. A distraction. A … snack. Still, they should've loaded themselves up with weapons inside. Magic was all well and good, but so was a blade.

Jack turned to tell Ozma as much and froze. She stood calmly in front of the open door with blue sparks flying from her hand. Large rips ran down the back of her dress, the frayed edges moving with a force that seemed to be coming from her body. Locks of her hair lifted and fell gently as the sparks became light that swept over her. A true *queen.*

"Ozma?" he asked in a dazed whisper. Was this supposed to be happening? She had the slippers so she would have her magic, but was this right? It looked … ethereal.

Then, her light exploded outward. Jack flung his arm up

against the brightness of it, squinting. A loud crack vibrated the ground as white-blue flames engulfed the Wizard's house.

I guess we're not getting a shit ton of weapons then…

Ozma turned toward him with a satisfied glint in her eye. The other was hidden behind a strip of fabric they had ripped from the furniture coverings. Blood was already seeping through, the sight of it tearing at his heart. She hadn't complained, but it had to hurt like a bitch. And, more than that, Jack hated that Ozma seemed to lose something every time she regained what was rightfully hers. To regain her true body, she'd lost two years of her life to darkness. To regain her magic and her realm, an eye.

"Just in case," she said, peering at Oz's burning home.

Jack simply stared at her. The beauty of Ozma stole his ability to think. To speak. She was extraordinary… And too good for him. She had chosen him, though, and he wasn't stupid enough to let his lack of self-worth ruin that.

"One more thing before we go." Ozma stepped closer and two shadows emerged behind her. "I want you to see them."

Jack's jaw dropped at the sight of her elegant, feathered wings. The iridescent sheen glistened in the fading firelight as she flexed them wide. "Shit," he breathed. Something inside of the house exploded, interrupting his fascination, and they both ducked, his ears ringing. "*Shit!* We need to get to the ship. Can you fly?"

"I don't know, but it doesn't matter. We're sticking together."

Ozma reached out for his hand with her own and he clasped it. Together they bolted back into the forest. His leg throbbed with each loping step. The wound on his thigh burned and stretched, but they had to get to Tik-Tok's ship before they were trapped.

Jack took comfort in knowing that Ozma could *feel* her way back to the shore, because he still felt slightly disoriented. The spell the Wizard had cast on him was broken but the effects seemed slow to fade. With the buzz in his head and the revelation of Ozma's power—her *wings*—Jack needed a minute to collect himself before putting his brain to work.

Growls reached their ears every so often—a grave reminder of the danger they were still in. After running for what felt like hours, the pain in Jack's leg forced them to stop and he lay down in the dirt, breathing heavily. "Sorry," he muttered to Ozma. She had to be in worse pain than he was after what she'd suffered with her eye.

"Don't be." She sat beside him and adjusted the stained cloth. He had stuffed extra strips in his pocket for when it needed refreshing.

I should've grabbed some for myself, he thought as he pushed aside the rip in his pants to see the wound. It was red and angry and far too deep. One of the brownies on board the ship would hopefully know how to stitch him up.

The snap of a twig sent both Jack and Ozma to their feet. *Oh, come on! Can't I get a moment?* A nude, rotting human female stumbled toward them through the trees. Her left arm hung by a few tendons, intestines bulging from a hole in her stomach. Two more silhouettes moved behind her.

Ozma lunged forward, kicking Oz's head where it lay on the ground. It sailed through the air, spinning as it went, and whizzed past the woman's ear. The female whirled around and chased after it.

"Hurry," Ozma said, and Jack obeyed.

When they finally reached the sandy shore again, Jack expected to be surrounded by enemies. He would've questioned the lack of monsters earlier if he realized how close they'd gotten to the water. But, instead of finding a hungry horde ready to tear them apart, dozens of bodies greeted them. They were spread across the beach, limbs twisted, with black liquid oozing from their orifices.

"What the hell?" he asked.

Ozma tugged him across the sand. "Don't question it. Let's just go."

She was right—it didn't matter, as long as they got out of there in one piece. Jack ushered Ozma into the row boat that was left for them and shoved it into the glistening silver water. Once it was far enough out to float, he jumped in beside her. Gentle waves bobbed them up and down while Jack gathered the oars, reminding him how ill he'd felt the last time they were on Tik-Tok's ship. He squinted through the bright moonlight at the hulking shadow of a ship. *Fuck.* It was better than being stuck in Orkland though, so, resigned, he rowed toward the pirates.

"How's your leg?" Ozma asked as he pulled the oars. "I can row if—"

"I'm fine," he assured her. *Or I will be.* As soon as someone took a needle and thread to him. And gave him the largest bottle of ale available—mostly to drink, but also to disinfect the cut.

Ozma pursed her lips. "You're a horrible liar."

He smirked. "I'm an astounding liar, Blossom. You just know me too well."

"I do," she agreed and glanced over her shoulder at the ship. "Why does it still feel so far away?"

Because we're both fucking exhausted.

But he kept rowing. If he stopped, even for a moment, he wasn't sure that he would find the strength to start again.

"You're alive." Tik-Tok popped his head over the side deck when they reached *The Wizard.* "And they say there's no such thing as a miracle."

Fucking asshat. "Just throw us a rope or something."

A rope ladder almost immediately fell and slapped against the side of the ship. Jack grabbed the ladder and held it steady for Ozma. She climbed ahead of him, her wings spread wide as if helping her balance, and he scrambled up behind her.

Once on the deck, Jack collapsed to his knees and sucked in the salty air. *Safe.* Or, relatively. Tik-Tok was still suspicious as fuck and he knew from books that the sea was fickle. No one greeted them with weapons though, so it was a good start.

"Wings, eh?" Tik-Tok leaned nonchalantly against the side

of the ship, staring at Ozma. His gaze landed on the bloody cloth covering her eye for a moment before returning to the feathered wings behind her. "Interesting."

"We'll be taking your quarters." Ozma's tone brokered no room for argument.

Tik-Tok lifted one brow. "You know, the last fae to have wings like *that* was a royal."

"Don't act like we didn't tell you who she was," Jack snapped.

"Oh, please." Tik-Tok rolled his eyes. "If I had a coin for every fae claiming to be a true heir, I could dock my ship for life. But if you were going to kill the Wizard, I didn't give two shits who you were. Whatever allowed me to start calling my ship by her rightful name again and get the fuck away from Orkland. *The Temptress* sounds more pleasant to the ears than *The Wizard*, doesn't it?"

Ozma ignored his comment about his ship's name. "Why make that deal with me, then? For the unborn child?"

"Bad odds are still odds, Your Highness." He tossed a key at her and gave a flourishing bow. "My rooms are yours until we reach the mainland."

"A healer." Jack got to his feet and stumbled slightly. "And food."

"Is that a request?" Tik-Tok asked. He caught a brownie by the back of her shift. "Hoist the anchor."

"A demand," Jack clarified. "Something substantial."

He laughed. "You're on a pirate ship, my grungy little carrot." Then he strode across the deck, stopping crewmembers every so often to bark out an order. "Kaliko! See to their wounds."

An older brownie with crooked fingers hobbled over, gave them each a once over, and made a soft *hmm* sound. "Don't move."

As if he had anywhere to go besides Tik-Tok's quarters. Still, he plunked down on a large wooden barrel and waited. Ozma did the same, tucking her wings into her back. The brownie returned with a leather sack a few minutes later.

"I can't say this won't hurt," he said, plunging his hand inside the sack.

"Wonderful," Jack mumbled. Then a splash of liquid hit his wound and he clenched his jaw tight to keep himself from screaming.

Ozma wrapped her hand around his and gave a reassuring squeeze. He forced a smile for her benefit and swallowed a groan as the brownie began poking at the skin around the gash. However painful it was for him, her eye would be worse.

"You should drink this now so it starts working while I stitch this one up," the brownie said to Ozma. He tossed a bottle at her. "It'll numb you up."

"I don't get any?" Jack asked.

The brownie scowled as he resumed his painful examination. "It's a flesh wound."

I'll show you a flesh wound.

The first prick of the stitching needle stopped him from saying so. It was best not to anger the fae already stabbing him with a pointy object.

After the brownie had attended both their wounds, stitching his leg and redressing Ozma's eye, he gave them both vials of medication to take. The pain lessened shortly after and they were shown to Tik-Tok's private bathing chamber. It was small and held only the essentials, but they were clean. And *starving.*

"Come on, Jack," Ozma said gently.

He followed her to the captain's quarters and, when she locked the door behind them, lights flickered to life as if sensing their presence. The warm cinnamon scent reminded Jack of the farm—of pumpkin pies and cakes and cookies. A large desk took up the center of the room with two chairs in front and one behind. The dark wooden seats were partially covered in red velvet with gold studs. Trapped beneath a piece of glass on the desk was a map, and more hung on the walls. A white, half-dead flower sat in a vase on the windowsill, and the other side of the room was made of cupboards that stretched into the back of the space. There, white gauze curtains swept over a large corner bed.

Jack went to the cupboards first and opened them until he found what he wanted—a glass decanter and two glasses. He poured them each a decent amount. "A celebratory drink," he told Ozma when she joined him. He really just wanted to slow his racing thoughts enough to dull the adrenaline rush.

Ozma opened a few cupboards until she found a wedge of cheese and bread. "This is probably the best meal we'll find for now."

Jack's stomach growled loudly and he chuckled. "It seems you brought me back with a real appetite."

She stepped closer, holding the food in her hands, and stretched up to kiss him. Jack kissed her back, set the glasses down, and pulled her to his chest in one fluid movement. Their lips came frantically together, gliding, their tongues colliding. It almost felt like another battle—though this one promised a pleasurable ending. Jack groaned into Ozma's mouth, hunger forgotten, or rather, a new one taking shape.

The bread and cheese thumped to the ground as Ozma tugged at his clothes. "I need you inside me. And I know the position I want. Don't be sweet about it." She released him and slid her dress over her head, exposing her perfect breasts and every other inch of her.

"You don't have to tell me twice, Blossom." He didn't think he had it in him to be *sweet* at the moment anyway. Hell, he didn't even have the patience to remove his own damn clothing.

Jack spun her around and bent her over the desk. The twitch of his cock reminded him how desperately he needed the release. He gripped her naked hips, his fingertips digging into her soft flesh.

"I love you," he rasped.

"Show me how much." She panted, looking at him over her shoulder with a lust-filled eye.

Jack grinned and quickly released his cock. In one motion, he slid inside her, and could have come right then. But he held back and began thrusting at a fervent pace. She pushed against him, matching his rhythm, her tight ass slapping him, her firm breasts bouncing. The desk scraped back and forth across the floor with each push.

"You feel so good." Jack leaned down so his chest was against her warm back, and he nipped at her ear. A moan escaped her as he let go of one hip to circle her clit with his fingers. Again and again, he stroked. "Fuck."

Without warning, her core contracted around him and she gasped his name, still moving rhythmically along with him. The sensation built and built until it pulled him completely over the edge and he groaned, "Demand this any time you want, Blossom. Any time." Jack collapsed over her and kissed her neck.

"Do you think they heard us?" Ozma asked.

Jack chuckled into her hair. "They definitely did."

Ozma arched back as if she wanted to stand, so Jack slid away. She threw her head back and laughed.

"Care to share the joke?" Jack asked, already smiling over the infectious sound.

Ozma pressed a soft kiss to his lips. "We're alive."

"Indeed."

Ozma reached around him and grabbed the drinks. "To the Land of Oz."

"To *us*," Jack corrected, clinking his glass against hers.

"To us." She grinned and yanked at his shirt with her free hand. "Now let's get out of these clothes."

When Jack stirred awake a few hours later, his stomach queasy but full of bread and cheese, he focused on the female in his arms. Ozma's long lashes swept across her cheekbones as she slept, and her lips parted ever-so-slightly. He brushed a stray piece of hair from her forehead and replaced it with a kiss. *I love you.* He didn't speak the words, not wanting to wake her just yet, but his heart swelled at the mere sight of her. There wasn't a day over the last two years that he hadn't wished to have his beloved back. Now that she'd returned to him, he would make up for each moment they'd spent apart.

With a quick flick of his magic, Jack called the dry, vine-like leaves of the dead flower toward him. They moved slowly, almost painfully, and Jack felt what very little life was left in them. He sent a silent apology through the bond and coaxed them into a twisted, three-ring circle.

Ozma stirred. "What's going on?"

Jack snatched the ring from the air and hid it in his palm. "Nothing. Why?"

"I can feel you using your magic," she mumbled against his bare chest.

"We're giving that ring back to Tik-Tok," he grumbled.

She laughed. "You don't want to share with me? I'm sure it works both ways."

"We're giving it back," he insisted jokingly. "How am I to surprise you with anything if you can tell every time I grow a flower?"

Her blue eye slid up to meet his hazel ones. "Surprise?"

Jack licked his lips. "A question, really…"

Oh gods. His hands shook. *What if she says no?*

"A question?" She pushed up onto one elbow, her hair gliding over her bare breasts.

"You know I love you." He cleared his throat. "I'd do anything for you."

"And I you," she said, brows lowered in confusion.

"So, I was wondering… Or… Hoping, really…" *Spit it out, idiot.* He held his hand up between them and uncurled his fingers to reveal the ring. "Will you marry me?"

Ozma blinked down at his offering.

Seconds ticked by without an answer and Jack nearly jumped out of his skin. "I'll get you a better ring."

"No!" She snatched the twisted vines from his palm. "I want this one."

Jack's heart hammered in his chest. "Is … that a yes?"

"Yes." Ozma pushed the ring onto her finger and gripped his face. "Yes." She pressed her lips to his. "Yes." Climbing onto his lap, she showered him with kisses. "Yes, yes, yes!"

Jack let out a relieved breath and placed his head to her chest, listening to her heart beat. "Thank fuck."

They shifted together beneath the covers, pressing closer. Ozma avoided touching his injured leg and he gently shifted so her eye wasn't pressed into his arm. His cock stiffened again, but he shoved down the desire. For now, they needed rest. Forever lay ahead of them. A life together. Happiness. Everything they had always wanted and didn't know was possible. Until now.

Epilogue

Ozma

As Ozma and Jack drew closer to the Emerald City, she peered down at the ring on her finger that he'd crafted. It was perfect, and it would remain on that digit for as long as they lived. Beside it rested the gold token from Tik-Tok, a reminder of a debt that still needed to be paid. But for now, she would have to push that thought aside.

On their journey, Ozma had purchased a new dress from the market in Loland and a shimmery blue eye patch, along with some ointment for Jack's leg. She wasn't used to having one eye yet, but she would adjust. Jack had returned to their farm and gathered a few of his books and clothing before they'd departed again on foot. They didn't take any of the pumpkin seeds—they would rather plant new things at their secret house once they settled in at the palace.

Crossing the Shifting Sands had been much simpler with magic. The beasts had remained hidden when Ozma sparked her blue power to life, willing it to create a barrier of protection.

Jack wrapped one arm around her waist as they walked the yellow brick road and brushed her hair aside with the other. He gently kissed his way up her neck, and she could feel every inch of his strong body behind her. His warm breath caressed her ear as he spoke, "Are you going to try and fly yet?"

She had told Jack she would attempt it once they reached the outskirts of the Emerald City. Her wings were still too new, and she didn't know if they were strong enough to lift her yet.

"Fine." Whirling around, she circled her arms around his neck. "But catch me if I fall."

"The branches will be ready." He flicked his tongue over her lips. "However, you won't need them."

Closing her eye for a brief moment, she let the magic stir, the blue energy raging inside her. Her wings released from her back, the wind from the movement rumpling Jack's hair. This time she was able to use her magic so her clothing wouldn't shred.

Ozma took a step back from him, pumping her wings, once, twice, until her feet lifted from the ground into a wide-open space.

As though she'd always had them, Ozma flapped her new appendages, going up and up until she was near the tops of the trees.

Jack's hand hovered at his forehead, blocking the sun, as he watched her in the air. "See! You don't need my help, Blossom."

Slowly, she retreated back to the ground, her silver slippers crunching the leaves. She stumbled forward and Jack caught her around the waist.

"Or maybe you do, just a bit." He smiled the brightest of smiles. "Ever since I've known you, you've been beautiful, but you've never been more radiant than you are now."

She pressed her lips to his, tasting the fruit he'd eaten earlier. "Tonight, pick your pleasure, and I'll do what you ask."

His pupils dilated. "Yes, my queen."

Ozma chuckled and tugged him forward so they could head into the Emerald City. The journey through the East had been quiet during the nights, not a single sound from the cursed pixies. Reva must have defeated Locasta—she could feel it all the way down to her bones.

Beneath their feet, the yellowed bricks became a sparkly shade of green as they entered the Emerald City. She watched Jack peer around at the crumbled buildings with wide eyes. Her heart accelerated, not at the destruction, but because there were fae outside repairing the broken architecture. Hammering, sawing, painting. The Emerald City beat like a heart inside her veins with each step, drawing her closer and closer to its center.

Ozma looked at the different shops—broken windows being replaced at a bakery, a new door being put in at a flower shop, and fabrics being carried from wagons into a building. Each street they walked was bustling with renewed life.

Eventually, they rounded a corner and Ozma held back a gasp. There it stood—the palace. Even from a distance, she knew it wasn't in perfect condition. There were holes in the green walls and blackened areas that would need to be mended. Even though it was in need of repair, it had the potential to be glorious.

"Sure you don't want to turn around?" Jack teased.

"We're used to a little hard work." Ozma rolled her eyes.

The palace door swung open and two guards walked out from the building: one male fae with long silver locks cascading down his back and the other with feathers intertwined in his obsidian hair. No, not guards—she *recognized* them.

Tin and Crow.

The silver-haired fae focused first on Jack and lifted his axe, his face like stone. Jack was already raising his hand in defense, then Tin's gaze shifted to Ozma. His expression didn't soften, but he gave a brief nod as he lowered his axe a fraction.

"Quit being an ass," Crow grunted to Tin. He sauntered toward Ozma. "You made it just in time. We were going to leave in a couple days to search for you. There were guards under oath to the Wizard, stuck here by that bond, but then a few days ago they were able to go home."

"Where's Reva?" Ozma rushed out the words, moving toward the palace.

"She's not in there." Crow tilted his head in the direction behind her. "But she's coming this way."

Ozma whirled around, spotting three fae in the distance. Thelia, who wore a lavender dress and her brown hair pulled into a single braid, with a young faun beside her. On her other side was Reva, dressed in her usual black, her long sleek hair falling to her waist.

"Did it work out for you two?" Ozma whispered to Crow.

"The entire palace can hear them fucking almost every night, so I'd say so," Tin grunted.

"Fuck off." Crow fought a smile.

"Ozma?" Reva shouted. Her friend took off at a sprint, leaving Thelia and the faun behind. Once she was close enough, Reva threw her arms around Ozma, squeezing her so hard she could barely breathe.

With a smile, Ozma returned the hug.

Reva froze when she pulled back, a horrified expression crossing her face. "Why are you wearing an eye patch?"

"One of us was bound to lose an eye." Ozma tried to make her voice sound light, but rushed to change the subject. "I heard the good news about you and Crow, and I suppose you have me to thank for him catching up to you."

"I should have known he had some help." Reva's gaze slid to Crow, a smirk forming on her lips.

"It isn't as though I wouldn't have found you anyway," Crow said with a wink.

"We had a little help from the Gnome King." Reva fished something out of her pocket and tossed it in the air. "We killed that bastard, too."

Ozma could only focus on the shiny red stone shaped like a heart. Her lips parted, and she snatched the stone before Reva could catch it.

"Where did you get this?" she asked, her voice shaky. The last time she'd seen it was when she'd given it to Tik-Tok.

"From the Gnome King's chest." Reva shrugged. "Whatever

spell turned the Gnome King to stone apparently also gave him a heart that prevents curses."

Ozma clenched her teeth. Tik-Tok had known the entire time what she'd held, and he hadn't said anything. But why would he? "Mombi had one and I traded it." She handed the stone back to Reva.

"The Gnome Queen's heart," Crow said softly. "That's where it was."

"Now it's with a pirate named Tik-Tok." Ozma sighed. A rush of anger fired up in her. She could have used that stone against the Wizard if she'd known sooner. Though she'd defeated him anyway, she still couldn't help feeling a little bitter about it.

Reva narrowed her eyes. "I know Tik-Tok. He's a sneaky, cocky bastard, but he shouldn't be a threat."

Yet he would be a threat for someone… One day.

"Glad you made it," Thelia said, strolling up with the faun. "This is Birch. Part of my new guard." The youngling straightened his spine and lifted his chin, his small antlers peeping out from his hair.

Ozma could feel Tin rolling his eyes behind her.

"You will do well in keeping Thelia safe." Ozma smiled and locked her gaze onto Thelia's brown irises. Taking a deep swallow, she glanced over her shoulder at Tin, at his silver hair. A nagging feeling washed over her—she quickly shook away the thought. It was just a coincidence. Lots of fae had silver hair and brown eyes.

"Please tell us the Wizard is just as dead as Locasta," Reva said.

A weight lifted off Ozma. The wicked had been defeated. All of them were now gone. That didn't mean that there weren't others out there who would attempt to rise, but the ones who had driven Oz into despair were gone. "The Wizard and Mombi are both slain."

"Fuck yes." Reva grasped Ozma by the shoulders and

smiled. "We did this." She spun and looked at everyone standing there. "We all did."

They all smiled back, except for Tin, who appeared as though he were done with this conversation.

"It was a bitch removing the spell from the palace that was suppressing our magic," Reva continued, "but Thelia helped me wipe it out. A protective barrier from King Pastoria remains, though. Has your magic returned?"

Pastoria—her father whom she would never know. At least part of him was still here. Ozma lifted her hands and called on her power. The blue glittery fire rocketed through her until two orbs of flame rested on her hands. She quickly flexed her spine, the wings shooting out from her back.

"I have to say I'm envious." Reva chuckled. "It's beautiful."

"She is," Jack finally spoke. And all eyes turned to him.

"This is my Jack." Ozma grabbed his tunic sleeve and tugged him closer. "He's going to be my husband."

"A wedding!" Thelia clapped her hands together.

"Before we start discussing wedding plans," Ozma started, "I think we'd better talk about our next steps in rebuilding Oz."

"The three of us together, ruling, will become enough," Reva said.

"It will remain enough," Thelia added.

"It will forever be enough." Ozma sucked in a breath of true victory. They'd all been a part of liberating their world. Now, she and Jack were both free, and, with their freedom, they had still chosen each other. Soon, the rest of Oz would know what it meant to be truly free too.

Ozma turned to her beloved, his smile mirroring hers when she said, "Welcome home, Jack."

Did you enjoy Ozma?

Authors always appreciate reviews, whether long or short.

Want more Faeries of Oz? Check out Tik-Tok, Book Four, in the Faeries of Oz series!

North has tried her whole life to pave her own path, to break free from the shadows of the most powerful fae in Oz. Being born without magic of her own makes it difficult, but she still has the love of her life in her corner. Or, at least, until she learns that he doesn't return her feelings, ripping a gaping hole in her heart.

Tik-Tok does what he wants, says what he wants, and rules how he wants. The sea has been his home—his—except when he was begrudgingly bound to serve the now-dead Wizard. But even after decades of freedom, he is still without the one thing he needs: the prophesied female who can open portals through the sea. Without her, he can't fulfill his destiny.

When Tik-Tok finds North—the fae he's been waiting for—he wastes no time stealing her away. He isn't expecting to fall in love with her, perhaps a quick tumble, sure, but nothing more. However, a past he is forced to confront may do more than haunt him … it may destroy North.

Also From Candace Robinson

Glass Vault Duology
Quinsey Wolfe's Glass Vault
The Bride of Glass

The Laith Trilogy
Clouded By Envy
Veiled By Desire
Shadowed By Despair

Faeries of Oz Series
Lion (Short Story Prequel)
Tin
Crow
Ozma
Tik-Tok

Cursed Hearts Duology
Lyrics & Curses
Music & Mirrors

Letters Duology
Dearest Clementine: Dark and Romantic Monstrous Tales
Dearest Dorin: A Romantic Ghostly Tale

Campfire Fantasy Tales Series
Lullaby of Flames
A Layer Hidden
The Celebration Game

The Bone Valley
Hearts Are Like Balloons
Bacon Pie
Avocado Bliss

Also From Amber R. Duell

The Dark Dreamer Trilogy
Dream Keeper
Dark Consort
Night Warden

Forgotten Gods
The Last Goodbye (Short Story Prequel)
Fragile Chaos

Faeries of Oz Series
Lion (Short Story Prequel)
Tin
Crow
Ozma
Tik-Tok

Darkness Series: Temptation
Darkness Whispered

When Stars Are Bright

Acknowledgments

Thank you so much to all the readers who have stayed with us on this Oz journey! We hope you've loved the characters and the retellings of them!

To our families and friends, you guys are the best! We'd like to give big hugs to Elle, Tracy, Amber H., Donna, Lauren, Lindsay, Jenny, Loretta, Victoria, and Ann for making this last book amazing. You guys are wonderful and we couldn't do it without you all.

Ozma and Jack's story was one of our favorites to write, and we would love for you to message us and let us know who your favorite characters from the entire series is!

About the Authors

Candace Robinson spends her days consumed by words and hoping to one day find her own DeLorean time machine. Her life consists of avoiding migraines, admiring Bonsai trees, watching classic movies, and living with her husband and daughter in Texas—where it can be forty degrees one day and eighty the next.

Amber R. Duell was born and raised in a small town in Central New York. While it will always be home, she's constantly moving with her husband and two sons as a military wife. She does her best writing in the middle of the night, surviving the daylight hours with massive amounts of caffeine. When not reading or writing, she enjoys snowboarding, embroidering, and snuggling with her cats.

Apple of Fate by Elle Beaumont

Acontius desires the one thing in life he can't have–a soul mate. Raised by the Greek goddess, Artemis, Acontius swore an oath to serve her for eternity, and abstain from love.

Centuries later, when Olympus has fallen and the gods live amongst humankind, Acontius discovers a young woman who mirrors his loneliness and longing. Throwing caution to the wind, he tosses an apple at her feet, engraved with words that bind them to one another.

Delia's life is in shambles. She's just lost her job, suffered through a recent breakup and her health is declining. What she needs more than ever is a getaway trip to another country. But when she meets a playful museum worker, Delia decides to let her walls down for once, which unwittingly sparks a goddess's ire.

With Delia's life hanging in the balance, Acontius must ensure she falls in love with him—or else she'll die and he'll become another one of Artemis' hunting dogs for eternity.

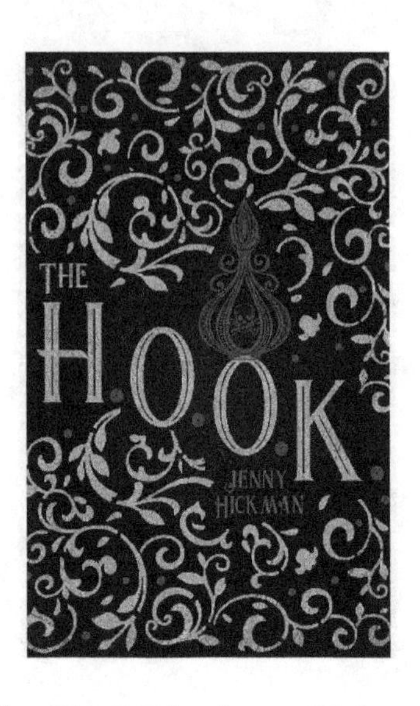

The HOOK by Jenny Hickman

Tomorrow isn't promised, no matter how immortal you think you are.

In the aftermath of Vivienne's capture, she discovers she's destined to become one of the Forgetful P.A.N. The devastating diagnosis leaves her questioning her relationships—and her place in Neverland. While on her second recruitment mission, she ignores a cardinal rule, and one of her fellow P.A.N. pays the ultimate price for her mistake.

Outrage over the death spurs Lee Somerfield's growing rebellious faction to fight fire with fire, leaving H.O.O.K. in ashes and Neverland ripped apart from within.

Navigating new love and old secrets, Vivienne must now face the consequences of her actions … and decide if living forever is worth forgetting everything.

CPSIA information can be obtained
at www.ICGtesting.com
Printed in the USA
BVHW031334230122
626777BV00014B/44